Lover's Remorse

2

NIA RICH

Also by Nia Rich

Never Going Back

My Love Is Deeper

F--k Boy

Triangles

Seduced by a Savage

Lovers Remorse 2

Written by: Nia Rich
Copyright © 2017 Nia Rich

All rights reserved.

Cover: Tina Louise
Editor: Venitia Crawford

Previously in Lovers Remorse…
Angel

Angel decided to hang out with Tanisha instead of with her husband and the guys for the Super Bowl. Her husband was at his brother's Super Bowl party like he was every year. Royce was with the guys at his place like he was the year prior. Tanisha and Angel were hanging out at her apartment. They were watching the first season of her favorite drama series Queen Sugar.

Tanisha was single, and she lived alone with a cute little dog that barked too much. Angel was relieved that Tanisha didn't have any plans and invited her over. She didn't feel like hanging out with Lucky acting like everything was alright and it wasn't. Angel was letting

Tanisha flat iron her hair while they were watching the show.

"Have you been feeling any morning sickness?" Tanisha asked.

"No. I've been extremely tired though."

"Yea. I know how that is."

"How do you know when you don't have any kids?"

"I've never told you that I had a still born baby when I was twenty-one years old. Me and my ex-boyfriend were devastated. I have her name tattooed on my arm."

"I've always wondered whose name that was on your arm. I didn't want to be rude and ask."

"Yup. We broke up shortly after that. He went on to have two kids. I don't think I ever recovered from it. My last boyfriend wanted a baby, but I couldn't bring myself to do it again."

"I understand. That is a hard pill to swallow."

"It was. I always remember holding my dead baby in my arms. Anyways let me not scare you. You are going to have a beautiful, healthy baby, and I can't wait to see him or her. Do you know what you want?"

"A girl, but I'll be happy with either."

She looked at the television and said, "Ralphangel does not need to get back with her."

She was referring to one of the characters on the show. Angel laughed, and then she said, "I found a house."

"Really? Where?"

"In Chandler. The asking price is a little high, so I'm negotiating to bring it down. It's the one that I told you about a few weeks ago. I hope I get it. If not, there is another one that I liked in Phoenix."

"Girl I'm so excited for you!" Tanisha said.

"Thank you! I am happy to start this new chapter in my life and close the old one."

"I know you are."

"Royce and I have talked about living together a few times now. Both of us are ready to live together. We're tired of living separately and we're ready to build a home together and be a family. We both want a traditional household. You know, house, family, and dog. We plan to buy a puppy when the baby is born so they can grow up together. We also want to host holidays at our house."

"Aww that is cute." Tanisha said.

Angel heard her phone ringing and said, "Tanisha can you hand me that."

"Yup." Tanisha put the flat iron down and reached behind her to take Angel's phone off the charger.

"It's Lucky." Tanisha said when she handed the phone to Angel.

Angel rolled her eyes and answered the phone, "Hey Lucky."

"Hey baby. I need you to do something for me. I forgot the meatballs you made for us at the house on an accident. You're closer to the house than I am. Can you please stop by there and bring them over here? The guys are asking about your famous meatballs and they are pissed at me for forgetting them."

"You can't go get them Lucky?" she asked.

"No because if I go now, I am going to miss most of the game. Baby please."

Angel rolled her eyes and said, "Alright. I'm on the way." She hung up the phone and let out an irritable sigh.

"Do you want me to ride with you? I don't have shit to do." Tanisha said as she finished flat ironing the last piece of hair.

She combed through her flat ironed style, and then Angel stood up and walked over to the mirror.

"Girl this looks good. You should have been a hair stylist." Angel said.

"Thank you. I thought about going to beauty school a few times, but I never pursued it." Tanisha said.

"You would make a killing with these kinds of skills." Angel said as she played around with her a little.

Angel walked away from the mirror, picked up her purse and phone, and then Tanisha followed her out of her apartment door.

***

"Girl, I forgot how big your house is." Tanisha said when they walked into Angel and Lucky's home. She followed Angel to the kitchen.

"I know. Too big. I am going to miss it, but I don't want to fight over it. If he wants it, he can have it."

"Girl you're a good one because I wouldn't let him have my house. Especially not this one."

"I hear you. I am ready to downsize anyway." Angel said.

"I can move here, and you can have my apartment if you want something smaller."

Angel laughed and said, "Be quiet girl. Would you like some water?"

"Yes."

Angel pulled two bottles of water out of the fridge and handed Tanisha one. Angel picked up the pan of meatballs from the island counter, and then they left Angel's house.

It didn't take them long to make it to Lucky's brother's house in Phoenix. They pulled into the driveway and got out. Angel got the pot of meatballs from the back seat and Tanisha followed her up to the door. They rang the doorbell and Lucky answered the door.

"Hey baby! Hey Tanisha!" Lucky said when he opened the door. He was lively per usual on Super Bowl Sunday.

"Hi Lucky!" Tanisha said.

"Thank you so much baby!" he said.

He kissed Angel on the cheek, took the pan of meatballs out of her hand, and said, "Come in and say hi to everyone!"

"No baby we are going to get going." Angel said.

She didn't want to get sucked into the Super Bowl excitement, and then get stuck over there with Lucky and all his friends and family. She wanted to get out of there.

"Aw baby you can't leave without speaking. That is rude." Lucky said.

Angel rolled her eyes and said, "Ok."

Tanisha and Angel followed him inside. She heard people cheering at the television as they turned the corner into the den. That is where everyone watched the game every year. Her plan was to say hello to everyone, and then get out of there quick.

"Everyone this is my wife Angel, and this is her friend Tanisha." Lucky said loudly.

Everyone smiled and spoke to them, and then her husband's brother Henry walked over, gave her a hug, and then he took the pan of food from her husband's hands. Angel smiled, waved, scanned the room to see who was there, and then she paused when she made eye contact with Royce.

Royce.

"Oh, my God!" she thought.

Royce was there sitting on the couch. Royce's eyes were locked on her. Angel was frozen. She heard everyone talking, but it felt like everything had stopped. The look in Royce's eyes told her everything he was thinking. Angel felt like her heart had stopped beating. She couldn't breathe, so she smiled, did a quick wave, and then she grabbed Tanisha's hand and headed back to the door.

"Damn baby you didn't even kiss me." Lucky said with a laugh.

"Ten years of marriage and I can't even get a kiss goodbye." Lucky joked loudly. Angel heard people laugh as she was walking out.

Lucky stopped Angel at the door, and asked, "Baby why are you leaving so fast? Give me a kiss."

Angel turned, kissed him quickly, and walked out of the door.

Lover's Remorse

2

NIA RICH

Nia Rich

Royce

Chapter 1

Royce

A couple of days earlier…

I heard a knock on my office door.

"Come in!" I said.

"Hey brotha! How are you?" Clarence asked.

"I'm doing well. How about yourself?" I asked.

Clarence slapped hands with me, and then he sat down in my office chair.

"Doing good. Just coming to check on you. How is the new position going for you?"

"Very well, Sir." I said.

"That's good and you've been doing great. My boss has a lot of great things to say about you." he said.

"That is great to hear. Thank you."

"You're welcome. Just keep up the excellent work."

"I will." I said.

He reached over and shook my hand again, and then he said, "Ok enough about work. What's up with Super Bowl Sunday? Do you have any plans?"

"I usually have my guys over. Why what's up?"

"Well my brother usually has a huge party at his house. You should come through. There's going to be lots of food and beer man."

I rubbed my chin, and said, "Um, I don't know."

"Bring the fellas and come through. You don't want to miss out on all that good food I'm telling you. Plus, my wife and my sister-in-law usually invite their single friends over, so the ladies will be there."

"Aight, well, I'll let you know."

"Cool! I hope to see you. Well, I got a bunch of work to get done, so I'll talk to you later."

"Alright Clarence." I said.

I watched him walk out of the door, and then I turned to my computer to concentrate on my work. I wanted to get it done and get out of there, so I could meet up with my guys to play pool like I do every Friday evening.

***

"I'm not going to be over for the Super Bowl man. I gotta jet to Cali tomorrow morning." Greg said.

"Cali?" I asked.

"Yea I got some business to handle with my family out there." Greg said.

Darnell said, "I won't be there either bro. Baby mom's is forcing me to go to her dad's this year. She tryna get us to bond 'n shit. I told her that her dad ain't gonna like me no matter what I do, but she insists, so." Darnell shrugged his shoulders, and then he took a sip of beer.

Kevin said, "Yea, and I'm gonna be at home with my wife. She is pregnant and going through it, so I gotta stay by her."

"You didn't tell me that you had another baby on the way bruh. Congrats." I said, and then I slapped hands with him.

"Yea, congrats bruh!" Greg said.

"Congrats." Darnell said.

"Thanks. It's baby number three for us." Kevin said.

"Damn. You got a little village over there." Greg said.

Kevin laughed. "We don't have that many kids bruh, but I'm done after this."

Darnell said, "I hear ya. I can't even deal with my one, but three, bro? You're a good one."

Kevin said, "It takes a lot of patience, but my wife and I are a team, so we make it work."

"That's right." I said.

I gave Kevin a fist pound, and then I took a gulp of my beer. I wanted to tell them about me and Angel's baby, but I held my tongue like I promised her.

I said, "Looks like I'm going to be alone this year."

"Sorry about that bro." Darnell said.

"It's all good. My boss invited me to a Super Bowl party at his brother's house, so I might stop through there."

"Your boss?" Greg asked.

"Yea. He's a cool cat. A little wild, but we hang sometimes outside of work. He helped me get my promotion."

"He must be cool because I don't know too many people who hang out with their boss bruh." Greg said.

"Me either." Darnell said.

"He's straight. He keeps what we do, outside of work, so we're cool."

"That's cool. It's good to have friends in high places. You never know when you will need them." Kevin said.

"True." I said.

I took another swig of beer and put the mug on the table. I walked over to the pool table and took my shot. I knocked three solid balls in.

"Bout to take y'all money tonight." I said.

"Yea whatever." Greg said.

"What's up with the wedding bro? Did y'all start planning it yet?" Darnell asked.

"We are looking for a house right now. We are gonna start planning the wedding after that."

"Damn bruh. I didn't think that I would see the day that you would settle down." Greg said.

"Yea. How does Darnell say it? That's bae." I said. Darnell and Kevin started laughing.

"She got you sprung." Greg said.

"Call it what you want. I'm for real about this" I said.

"I can respect that bruh." Greg said, and then he slapped hands with me.

"All of you are gonna be my groom's men, right?" I asked.

"No doubt." Greg said.

"You know I got you." Kevin said.

"Absolutely." Darnell said.

"Bro you're gonna be my best man. Are you cool with that?" I asked Darnell.

"Hell yea." he said, and then slapped hands with me.

"Aight cool. I'm gonna let you all know when we start planning. It should be soon."

Everyone nodded their heads and got back to the pool game. We listened to Greg tell us another one of his elaborate stories about one of his chicks, and then we all went home.

Chapter 2

Royce

The day before...

"Hey baby." Angel said when she answered the phone.

"How's work?" I asked.

I looked outside my window at the mid-morning sun. Angel was at work on a Saturday per usual, and I was at home. I was sitting in front of my laptop getting some work done.

Angel said, "Busy. I am tired, and I have a lot of stuff to take care of when I get home, so I'm probably not going to be able to stop by tonight."

"That's cool baby. How are you feeling?" I asked.

"Besides being tired, I am alright. I miss you."

"I miss you too."

"Shoot Roy, I have to go. I have another client coming. I love you."

"I love you too."

We disconnected the call, and then I got back to work. There was a lot of work that I needed to get done before Monday. I put my eyes back on my laptop and zoned out for a while. Before I knew it, late afternoon had arrived. My mom called and asked me to stop by and help her with her new bookshelf, so I headed over to her house.

When I got to my mom's house, she had more than the book shelf that she wanted me to do. I ended up putting together a book shelf, fixing a door, hanging some pictures, rearranging her new furniture, and if that wasn't enough, she asked me to help her clean out her garage. I should have known my mom was going to put me to work. She knew that I was not going to tell her no, and I was the only one that would do it. Darnell never helped her with anything. He always had an excuse whenever she asked him to do anything. I hated that about him.

After my mother worked me to death, she fed me. She'd cooked up a bunch of soul food the day before, so she fixed me a huge plate and, sat down at the table with me.

"Thank you, son." my mom said.

"For letting you work me?"

"Well, I don't have anyone else around here to do it."

"Why don't you call dad?"

"I'm not calling that old fool." she said, and then I started laughing.

"So, how's your fiancé?"

"She's good. Working hard as usual."

"I really like her."

"Yea pops does too. She's a good girl."

"I can see that you really like her too. I've never seen you this way for any woman."

"I've never felt this way for any woman."

"That's sweet son. You remind me of your dad back in the days."

"Back in the days, huh?"

My mom laughed, and then she said, "Yes. Your dad was handsome, and all the girls wanted him, but he liked me. He was very picky with women. He would never deal with any 'ole thing running around. He said that he chose me because I was a good girl."

She stared off in space for a moment, and then she said, "Yea those were the good 'ole days."

"I don't understand why you and pop couldn't keep it together after all these years."

"People grow apart son. We held it together for as long as we could for you guys, but there was no sense in us carrying on once y'all were grown. I'm fine by myself. Plus, I have three sons to help me with stuff."

"One really."

"Awww don't be so hard on your brother's. Darnell comes over to help with stuff too. He just fixed the legs on this dining room table the other day, and he helped me set up my new cell phone," she said.

I made a screwed face at her. She laughed and said, "I know your brother is a knuckle head, but he is still my son and your brother.

"I hear ya mom."

"Um hum. Do you want me to put the rest of that food in a to-go container?"

"Yes, could you? I'm dead tired. You worked the mess out of me."

She laughed and said, "You're too young to be talking about your tired son."

She stood up slowly and took my plate and hers over to the kitchen counter. She opened the cabinet and pulled out a couple of Tupperware containers. She put the food from the plate into one of the containers, and then she filled the other container with food from the refrigerator.

"This one is for Angel." she said.

"Ok, thanks. She will love it."

She put both containers into a grocery bag and walked back over to the table. She handed the bag to me. I stood up, gave her a warm hug, and then I kissed her on the cheek.

"I love you mom. Thanks for the food." I said.

"I love you too Roy. Thanks for coming over to help an old lady."

I laughed and said, "Mom stop you're not old and you're beautiful." I rubbed her hair.

She smiled and said, "Thanks son. Call me to let me know that you made it home safe."

"I will.

Chapter 3

Royce

The night before...

When I got home, Angel's car was in the driveway. I smiled, hung up the phone with my mom, and walked inside. She wasn't downstairs, so I figured that she was in the bedroom. I stopped in the kitchen to put the Tupperware containers into the refrigerator. I walked back through my house and up the short flight of stairs to the third level. I smiled when I saw her sleeping in my bed. She had the cover pulled up to her neck. I walked up to her and kissed her on the cheek.

She woke up and said, "Hey baby. I wanted to see you before I went home. I was so exhausted. I needed to take a nap."

"Why didn't you tell me you were coming?" I asked.

"I wanted to surprise you. I was gonna be waiting naked for you, but as you can see, our baby wouldn't let me."

I chuckled, slipped off my shoes and climbed in the bed next to her. I hugged her and placed soft kisses on her lips.

"Where are you coming from?"

"My mom's"

"How is she?"

"She is good. Worked me to death. She asked about you."

"Oh really?"

"Yea. She said that she really likes you."

"Aw that is sweet." Angel smiled.

"Oh, before I forget, she gave me a plate of food to give to you. It is in the fridge."

"Tell her that I said thank you."

"I will. I got to go."

"Baby why?"

"Because I got to cook some stuff for my mom for tomorrow."

"Just cook it here."

"I thought about that, but everything is at my house."

"Ok. I can come with you."

"No babe. It's ok. Tanisha is spending the night to help, and then we will be going over there for the game. My mom is having a girl's night for the Super Bowl. No boys allowed. I will talk to her about meeting you while I am over there."

"Ok, well I'm making love to you first before you leave."

"When?"

"Right now."

"Stop playing."

"I'm not." I said.

She giggled as I lifted and climbed on top of her. I pulled the covers off her and discovered that she was nude underneath the entire time.

"You *are* naked." I smiled.

"I know."

"Little freak." I said.

She giggled. I stood up, took my clothes off, and then I climbed back on top of her. I sucked on her perfectly round, deep brown nipples, and then I buried my face in her sweet center. I didn't come up for air. I kept licking her until she busted, and I pushed my love deep inside her.

"Mmm baby," she moaned as I slowly pumped in and out of her.

"Baby this pussy good." I moaned as I continued to stroke her.

"Mmm yes Royce," she moaned as she got another orgasm.

I slowed down and let her get it. When she relaxed, I sped up again. I spread her legs open wide, so I could feel all of her. The sight of her brown skin, her holding her breasts in her hands, and the sex faces she was making made me bust faster than I wanted to.

"Shit Angel." I moaned as I released into her. I laid on top of her for a moment.

"Why you make me do that? Huh?" I asked through short breaths. She giggled and kissed me.

"You knew what you were doing." she said.

I chuckled, rolled off Angel, and laid on the side of her. She stood up, walked out of the room, and down the stairs. I heard the refrigerator open and close, and then she came back with two bottles of water. She handed one of them to me.

"Thank you, baby." I said as I cracked open the bottle of water.

I sat up in the bed and leaned my back up against the head board. I took a few gulps of the water. She drank a few gulps of hers, put the bottle on the dresser, and went into the bathroom to take a shower.

I sat there for a second, and then I said, "She ain't leaving without giving me some more."

I walked into the bathroom and stepped in the shower with her. She smiled and turned towards me and kissed me.

"We haven't taken a shower together in a while." she said.

"I know." I said as I poured some of her liquid soap into my hand.

I started rubbing the soap onto her wet skin. She did the same to me. As the soap lathered, I felt my manhood swell again. She must have had been thinking what I was thinking because she rubbed soap on my erection, rinsed me off, and then she bent down and put it in her mouth. I looked down and watched her soft lips slid up and down my manhood. I leaned my back against the shower wall and put my hand behind her head. She looked up at me as she sucked on me, slow, with no hands.

"Uh-uh. You're not about to make me cum fast again." I said.

I stopped her and helped her stand up. I bent her over and entered her from the back. She put her hands on the wall and let the shower water run over her hair as I stroked her. I kept her in that position the entire time. I don't know how long we were in the shower making love. All I know is, I got my just due for busting too fast the first time. When it was over, she was begging me to stop, and that was the only reason I did. I could have done it until the next morning. After we got out of the shower, she dried her hair, got dressed, kissed me goodbye, and told me she loved me. I passed out right after I heard her lock the door with her key.

Chapter 4

Royce

Super Bowl Sunday...

I woke up with a weird feeling in my stomach. The feeling that something wasn't right. Once I finished my morning workout, I took a shower, got dressed, and walked downstairs to the dining room. The feeling in my stomach still hadn't gone away, but I tried to shake it and start my day. I planned to spend the day getting some work done before the game.

I put my laptop on the dining room table, opened it, and turned it on. I walked over to my coffee maker on my kitchen counter and got a pot brewing. I hadn't heard from Angel yet, so I called her, but her phone went to voicemail. I knew that she would call back whenever she got a chance. I was still feeling strange, so I said a quick prayer and asked for it to go away while I was pouring my cup of coffee. I declared that the day was going to be a good day before saying Amen. I began making myself breakfast, and then my thoughts started flooding my brain.

Why wouldn't Angel tell me about the party at her mom's way before yesterday? Something doesn't sound right about that, and why would she come over here, fall asleep, and then go home. I'm her man, she could have gone home in the morning. She was acting like a woman who has a man to go home to. Wait. What am I tripping on? There's been plenty of nights that she has gone home in the middle of the night because she had to work the next morning. She always says it's easier to get dressed at home because she has everything there and her job is closer to her home. It would take her an hour to get to work from here, but Angel doesn't have to work today because it's Sunday. She could have cooked here. Maybe I'm just in my feelings. Angel wouldn't lie to me. We love each other too much for that kind of nonsense.

I grabbed my plate of food and my cup of coffee and walked over to my dining room table. I had never felt that way about Angel before, so I wasn't sure why my thoughts were getting the best of me that morning. Up until that day, I had never questioned anything that Angel did. I was alright with the way things were between us. I had never been the type of man to cuff a woman, and I like my space as well, so I never tripped about her going home all the time.

Maybe I am sprung like Greg said. Maybe I haven't been paying attention; I give her the space she needs. I don't hound her. I never question her, but maybe that is giving her room to do me wrong. Nah baby isn't built like that. She tells me everything. She wouldn't do me dirty. I've been trusting her this whole time, so why stop now?

My phone started ringing. I picked it up and saw the picture of Angel I had saved to it.

"Good morning baby." I said.

"Good morning." she said quietly. Her voice was close to a whisper.

"What are you doing?" I asked.

"I'm sitting on the back patio having a cup of tea. I'm about to get started."

"Why are you talking so quiet?"

"I'm just waking up baby. I'm still tired."

"Oh ok. Did Tanisha make it?"

"Yea she's in the guest room sleeping. We were up late cooking and talking."

"I love you."

"I love you more. I'm gonna call you a little later when we get closer to finishing."

"Ok."

We hung up. That uncomfortable feeling kept pulling and tugging on me. I tried to put my focus on my work, but after staring at the screen for a moment, I decided a change of scenery might help. I finished my breakfast and put my dishes in the sink. I carried my coffee cup and laptop down the short flight of stairs, through my man cave, slid open the patio door, and stepped outside. I turned to slide the patio door closed. I sat down in one of the chairs and put my cup of coffee and laptop onto the table. The sun rays were bouncing off the water in my pool. It was warm outside, but it wasn't too hot. There was no breeze, no sounds, and it was peaceful. I felt my nerves calming down a little in the noiseless, outdoor environment. I opened my laptop up and got to work.

A few hours later, the sun was high in the sky and the temperature had risen. I was sitting underneath my patio awning, and the dry desert heat was unbearable even in the shade. I knew that it was time to take a break from working and go back inside. I closed my laptop, cuffed it underneath my arm, picked up my empty coffee cup, opened the patio door, and walked back into my house.

Once inside, I walked back into the kitchen and put the cup in the sink. I set my laptop on the dining room table, and then my phone started ringing. I figured that it was Angel calling to let me know that she was finished cooking, but it was my brother Darnell.

"What's up?" I asked.

"Bro you gotta come over here. Baby moms is tripping, she took my car keys, and my house keys, and she tryna call the police on me." he said hastily.

Darnell sounded nervous and I could hear his baby's mother going off in the background. She was yelling at him and throwing things.

"Whoa. What happened?" I asked.

"We got into an argument and now she's losing it. Bro please come. I'm not tryna go to jail."

"Yo! Chill out!" he yelled.

"Don't tell me to fucking chill out! I'm tired of your shit D!" I heard her yell, and then I heard something hit the wall by him.

"Why the fuck you throwing shit at me!? Why are you acting out in front of our son!?" he yelled.

"I don't give a fuck! Get out!" she yelled back.

"Bro. Come now."

"Yea! Tell your brother to come and get you!" she yelled.

It sounded like they started tussling a little bit by the sounds on the phone, so I said, "I'm on my way."

I hung up the phone. I stuffed my car keys into my navy-blue basketball shorts, ran upstairs to grab my wallet off my dresser, put on a pair of sneakers and walked out the door.

***

When I got to Darnell's house, he was standing outside in the garage. He walked out of the garage and got in my car. His child's mother snatched the front door open and started throwing his shit out of the house. She was a short, petite, Hispanic girl with long light brown hair. She was feisty to be so little. They'd been together for three years and that was not the first time that I had to rescue him from one of their dramatic fallouts.

"Yea take your shit with you!" she yelled as she threw his stuff in the yard.

"Chill out!" he yelled back.

"Fuck you! I hate your brother Royce! Take his shit with you before I fuck him up!" she yelled.

I didn't respond to her. I was just watching the show with my eyebrows raised.

"Aye pull off bro." he said.

I pulled off and started driving down the street, and then I asked, "Damn bro. What did you do this time?"

"Man, she went through my phone and shit. I forgot to lock it. I was drunk. She got to tripping on me this morning about some text messages me and this freak were sending back and forth." he said as his rubbed his neck.

"Man look at this shit man. She done scratched up my neck and she fucking bit me when I was trying to get my keys from her."

He showed me the bite mark on his hand, and then I said, "Damn bro."

"I know. If I was a crazy dude, I would have beat her ass, but she knows I'm not built like that. Man, damn I wish I would have locked my damn phone."

"You and her always got something going on. Ain't you tired of arguing with her?"

"Man." he said, and then shook his head back and forth.

"Do you want to come to my house?" I asked.

"Nah take me to pops crib. I already called him and told him that I was coming."

"Aight."

I drove to south Phoenix near 16th and Baseline to my pops house. My pops lived in a small two-bedroom house in the middle of the block. I pulled into the driveway and parked. My brother and I hopped out, walked up to the door, and rang the doorbell.

"Come in!" Pops called out.

We opened the door and walked in. Pops was sitting in his leather lazy boy chair watching television.

"Hurry up and shut the door so you don't let my air out." he said.

Pops was always complaining about the air conditioning going out of the house, if you didn't close the door fast enough. Darnell and I walked in and sat on Pops couch.

"Sup pop?" I asked.

I look just like my dad. He is tall, slender, and dark skin with a bald head. He had developed a gut over the years and he had a silver beard. Darnell has some of pops features, but he looks more like our mom.

"What's up boys what's going on?" he asked.

"Nothing's going on with me pop." I said.

"What happened with you and you girlfriend D?"

"Man pop she got to tripping about some chick I was talking to. We started arguing. She flipped out and scratched me up, took my keys, bit me, and started throwing my stuff out." Darnell said.

He touched the scratches on the back of his neck again, and then he started to shake his head.

"What did I tell you about playing with these women man. You can't be doing that."

"I know pop."

"Hear me now. I've been there and done that son. That can turn ugly quick, like it just did. Now what would have happened, if you wound up putting your hands on her? You would have been locked away, and I am not trying to have two of my sons up in there. It's already bad enough that I got one up in there, and you're up in these streets just like your brother used to be, and you know that I don't like that." Pops said.

"I know." Darnell said.

"Aight. Well, just let her calm down son. She will be alright once she calms down. You can hang out here until she does. You can stay in the second bedroom if you need to stay over for a while."

"Thanks pop."

"How are you doing Roy?"

"I'm fine pop." I said.

"How is your girl? What's her name? Angel?"

"Yes. She is doing good pop." I said, and then I heard my phone. I pulled it out of my pocket, stood up, and walked outside to answer it.

"Hey." I said.

"Hey babe. We just finished cooking, so we're going to head over to my mom's house in a little bit. What are you doing?" Angel said.

"I'm hanging out with my brother and my pops. My brother got into something with his baby mom, so I had to pick him up and bring him to my dad's house."

"Is everything ok?"

"Yea everything is fine."

"Ok well I am going to get going. I will see you later."

"Ok."

I hung up the phone and went back inside my pops house. I sat down on the couch with my brother and got caught up on the conversation he was having with my dad. I joined in the conversation and all three of us talked for a while. When I looked at my phone again, it was early evening and I told my dad and my brother that I had to go. I asked my bother if he wanted to go to the party with me, but he declined. He said that one of his friends was about to pick him up. I left and went home to get dressed and head over to Clarence's brothers house. I planned to talk to Angel about the things that I was feeling after the game

Chapter 5

Royce

Super Bowl Party…

Hey brotha! Come on in!" Clarence said when he opened the door of his brother's house.

I walked in the door, and then Clarence shook my hand. He closed the door and told me to follow him around the corner. There were a bunch of people sitting in a large den area of the house eating and talking. There was music playing and the pre-game show was showing on a large flat screen television mounted to the wall. Clarence introduced me to his brother Henry, and a few other people at the party; including his brother's wife.

"Thanks for coming man. It's nice to meet you." Henry said while shaking my hand.

"Thanks. It's nice to meet you too."

"Clarence always has wonderful things to say about you, so anybody who is good with him is good with me." Henry said, and then he excused himself and walked into the kitchen.

"I'm glad that you came through Royce." Clarence said.

"Thanks for inviting me Clarence." I said.

"What team are you going for?" he asked.

"Oh, you already know what team I'm going for." I chuckled.

"The losing team brotha." he said.

"Yea we gonna see about that." I said.

"Aight brotha, we will. There is food on the table and drinks in the cooler. Help yourself and make yourself comfortable."

"Thanks." I said.

I saw him pull his phone out of his pocket and go into another area of the house. I walked to the table and looked at all the food. Everything on the table looked delicious. Henry's wife walked up to me while I was standing at the table looking at all the food.

"Royce, right?" she asked.

"Yes." I smiled.

"Welcome to our home. Everything on this table *is* delicious because me and Clarence's wife cooked all of it. Even the barbeque. So, don't be shy," she said and smiled.

I chuckled and said, "Ok."

"I know. Shameless plug." she laughed.

"There are some beers in the cooler. Let me know if you need anything." she said.

"Ok." I said, and then she walked away.

I piled up my plate with food, and then I walked over and found a seat on one of the couches. Henry's wife turned down the music, and then he turned up the television because the football game started. Everyone's attention turned towards the television.

About thirty minutes into the game, the doorbell rang. Henry's wife walked over to me and offered to take my empty plate. Clarence went to go answer the door. A few seconds later he walked back around the corner and said, "Everyone this is my wife Angel, and this is her friend Tanisha."

I saw Angel and her friend turn the corner right behind him. My heart stopped when I made eye contact with her. The word *wife* echoed in my head, but I was silent with my eyes glued to her.

"Wife?!" I thought.

I felt like I couldn't have heard what I thought I heard. There was no way he called my woman, my future wife, and soon to be baby's mother *his wife*. I felt my heart start beating rapidly, and then I felt my body temperature rise. I watched Angel waved to everyone and hurriedly walked away. I saw Tanisha follow her out, but I was still stuck.

I heard Clarence say, "Damn baby you didn't even kiss me. Ten years of marriage and I can't even get a kiss goodbye."

I heard people laugh, but I was too numb to make a sound. I felt frozen in time. I shook my head back and forth slowly. I was pissed. I stood up and headed towards the door. Clarence walked back around the corner after closing the door.

He asked, "Aye brotha you're leaving?"

I said, "Yea, something came up."

Before he could respond, I walked out of the door. I knew right then, the gut feeling that I had earlier that day was right. Angel was married, and to my boss at that.

Nia Rich

Angel

Chapter 6

Angel

"Oh, my God Tanisha! That was Royce!" Angel yelled when they got a couple of houses away from Henry's house. Angel's hands were visibly shaking, and she started having a panic attack. Her chest was tight, and a waterfall of tears were streaming down her face.

"I know." Tanisha said as she shook her head back and forth. "Calm down Angel. Pull over into that store parking lot over there."

Tanisha pointed to a strip mall with a Walmart store in it. Angel turned left, pulled into the Walmart parking lot, and then she parked. She buried her head into her hands and cried hysterically.

"What am I going to do?" Angel asked while sobbing.

"I don't know honey." Tanisha said. She started rubbing Angel's back. She was doing her best to console Angel, but Tanisha was also startled by the whole ordeal.

"How do they know each other?" Tanisha asked.

"I don't know." Angel cried loudly.

"Oh man."

"It's over. I know it. Royce is going to have nothing to do with me. I should have just told him the truth from the beginning Tanisha."

"I know. Calm down." Tanisha said as she continued to rub Angel's back.

Tanisha couldn't stop shaking her head back and forth. She was trying to find the words to say, but she was having a tough time. She looked out the window at the palm trees in the Walmart parking lot and fell silent for a moment.

"Damn this is messed up. Maybe you should try talking to him and explain your situation. Maybe he will hear you out and understand." Tanisha finally said after a few minutes of silence.

"Understand what? That I've been lying to him this entire time? That I have been living a double life? He will never forgive me." Angel said.

"Calm down honey. Let's go to my place. I will drive. Switch places with me." Tanisha said.

They got out of the car, walked around the car, and got back inside in opposite seats. They put on their seat belts, and then Tanisha pulled out of the Walmart parking lot. Angel continued to weep silently as she looked out the window. She still couldn't get her breathing under control. She felt like something was squeezing the air out of her chest and she could only take short breaths in between tears. Angel heard her phone ringing in her purse, so she pulled it out of her purse and looked at it.

"It's Royce." she said to Tanisha.

"Answer it." Tanisha responded.

Angel took a deep breath and answered the phone.

"Hello?"

"Where are you?" he asked.

"On the way to Tanisha's place."

"Meet me at the park by her house."

"When?"

"Now." he said, and then he hung up.

"What did he say?" Tanisha asked.

"He wants me to meet him at the park by your house. He is pissed off."

"Do you want me to come with you?"

"No. I will be ok." Angel shook her head back and forth. Her eyes filled with more water. She wiped the hot tears from her eyes and cheeks, and then she put the phone back into her purse.

Tanisha said, "I'm sorry Angel."

"This is all my fault. I should have been truthful from the beginning, and then I wouldn't be in this mess right now." she said while looking out of the window.

Angel sniffled a few times and wiped her tears again. She pulled down the visor mirror, so she could clean herself up a little before seeing Royce. Angel dried her tears with her hand, and then she reapplied eyeliner, mascara, and lip gloss. She could feel her hand still shaking a little bit. Angel finger combed her hair back into the style Tanisha had done for her. She closed the visor mirror and watched Tanisha pull into her apartment complex parking lot. Tanisha pulled up to her building and parked.

"Are you going to be ok girl?" Tanisha asked.

"Yes. I'll be fine." Angel said.

"Ok. Call me if you need me." she said.

"Ok I will." Angel said.

Tanisha reached over and gave Angel a tight hug, and then she got out of the car and walked towards her building. Angel got out of the car on the passenger side and walked over to the driver's side. She got in, put her seat belt on, put her car into drive, and pulled off.

Chapter 7

Angel

Royce was already sitting on a park bench when Angel pulled up. It was still day light outside, but the sun was beginning to set. She parked and got out of her car. Angel wasn't ready to face the truth. She was feeling queasy as she approached him. Royce looked extremely angry. He had his hands cupped in front of him, and he was staring Angel directly in her eyes with an emotionless expression on his face. He was grinding his back teeth together; making his jaw clinch tight. Angel stopped walking and stood in front of him.

"Hey Roy-" she started to speak, but he cut her off.

"Don't hey me Angel," he said angrily.

Angel inhaled, and then she exhaled slowly trying to brace herself for what was coming. She adjusted her stance, but her shoulders were slumped, and a look of sadness covered her face.

"When were you going to tell me that you are married? Never right?" he asked irately.

"I'm sorry." Angel said. She felt her eyes began to water. She tried to hold them back, so she tilted her head back and looked up at the sky, and then she looked back at Royce who was bouncing one of his legs furiously.

"You're sorry? For lying to me this whole fucking time!" he yelled.

"Please let me explain." Angel pleaded.

"I don't want to hear shit! Angel!" Royce yelled. His voice cracked. Angel could see his eyes start to water which made her tears forced their way out of her eyes.

"I see you put my ring back on. Where's the wedding ring I saw on your finger a little while ago?! You been living a double life this whole time! You got me out here looking stupid!" he yelled, and then he looked up at the sky and grabbed the bridge of his nose to stop himself from crying.

"It's not like that!" Angel yelled, she wiped a few tears that had fallen from her eyes.

Royce looked back at her and asked, "Then what is it like then!? Huh!? You're fucking him too!?"

"Royce-" she said, but he cut her off again.

"I don't even know why I asked you that. Don't answer because I don't care!" he yelled.

"No Royce, please listen!" Angel pleaded again.

"I don't want to hear shit you got to say!" He yelled, and then he paused and said, "You know what? Go ahead. Humor me." He made a hand gesture that meant he was giving her the floor.

"I've been unhappily married for years. I'm in the process of getting a divorce-"

Royce cut her off again and said, "And you want me to believe that shit!? You've been lying to me for a year Angel! And to top it off, he is my fucking boss! You had the nerve to have me in that man's house Angel!! Fucking you and sleeping in his bed! You don't see something wrong with that!? You got me introducing you to my family, and you knew that you belonged to someone else! I gave you the key to my fucking house! I've never done no shit like that with a woman before!"

"I never meant to hurt you!" Angel cried out, but it fell on deaf ears. Royce was too angry to hear her apology pleads.

"Is this the reason why you were going home every night!? Is the reason why you've been so reluctant to introduce me to your family!? Because I'm your fucking secret?! I'm basically your side dude, right?!" Royce hollered. His voice echoed through the park. He put his fingers in the corner of his eyes to stop his tears from falling.

Angel wiped more tears with the back of her hand and said, "Royce, I'm sorry! It's not what you think!"

Royce's face frowned back up before saying, "It's not what I think!? I don't want to hear shit else Angel! Give me my key to my house."

He put his hand out and waited for Angel to place his house key in it. Angel slowly opened her hand bag and pulled the key out.

"Roy please can we talk about this?"

"Talk about what Angel!? There ain't shit else to say! Give me the key!" he demanded, so Angel slowly walked over to him and put the key in his hand. He cuffed the key, stood up, and walked away.

"Royce!" Angel said as she followed him. He remained silent and kept walking.

"Royce. Baby let me explain." Angel cried.

Royce turned back to her and said, "Angel leave me alone. I don't want to hear what you got to say. I've heard enough, and I'm done."

Angel stopped following him. She watched him get into his car and pull away. Angel slowly walked back to her car with her head hung low. She got into her car and cried for a moment before going home.

***

Angel was happy to see that Clarence wasn't home when she got home. She felt heavy and sick, and she didn't want to be bothered. Angel turned on the tub to fill it with hot bath water. As the tub filled, she tried to call Royce, but he sent her call to voicemail. She put the phone on the counter and turned the tub off. She took her clothes off, slid down into the steamy water, and closed her eyes. Angel soaked and let her tears fall until the water cooled down, and then she cleaned up and got out. After she put her pajamas on, she heard Lucky walk in the door downstairs.

"Baby!" he called out.

"Yes." she responded dryly.

Angel heard him making his way up the stairs. Lucky walked in the room and smiled.

"Hey beautiful." he said, and then he kissed her on the cheek.

"Hey Lucky." she replied.

"Thanks for cooking. Everyone loved the food. Henry's wife told me to tell you thank you. I brought home some of the left overs."

"Ok." Angel said.

"My team won! I cleaned up in cash tonight!" he exclaimed.

"That's good."

"What's wrong?"

"Nothing. I am just exhausted from cooking all day. I am going to go to bed."

"Ok. Well I am going to go downstairs, and I will be back up in a little bit."

"Ok." Angel said. She turned and walked towards the bed. She heard him answer his phone.

"Hello? Did you see that game tonight man! Whoo! They killed! Ha-ha!" he said as he walked down the stairs.

Angel unlocked her phone and looked at the last text messages she got from Royce. He was telling her how much he loved her. That was earlier that day. At that moment, he hated her. Angel wiped a couple of tears, and then she locked the phone, blacked out the screen, put the phone on the nightstand, and closed her eyes.

Chapter 8

Angel

"How are you feeling girl?" Tanisha asked. She was standing in the doorway of Angel's office.

"I don't know." Angel said. Tanisha walked in, closed the door behind her, and then she sat down in the chair in front of Angel's desk.

"What did he say when you talked to him?" Tanisha asked.

"He was so mad T. He called me a liar and he made me give him his house key back."

"Whoa."

"I know."

"What are you gonna do?"

"I don't know."

"Girl I can't lie to you. This is a mess."

"I know."

"Maybe you should let Royce calm down, and then try to talk to him again."

"I don't know if he is ever going to talk to me again. I decided that I need to start preparing to be a single mom. This is not how I planned this." Angel said.

Her voice cracked, and tears started to burn her eyes. Tanisha stood up and handed her a few pieces of Kleenex, and then she walked around to Angel's side of the desk and hugged her.

"Girl it will be ok." Tanisha said.

Tanisha walked out of Angel's office to let her have some time to herself before she took her first client. Angel felt numb the entire day at work. She was working on clients, but she wasn't there mentally. She couldn't recall one conversation she had with any of her clients that day. All she could think about was going home and going to sleep.

As she drove past cactus's and palm trees on her way home from work, she thought about Royce. In a blink of an eye her life had changed for the worse, and it happened right when she thought that she had everything under control. Angel had always been taught that what was done in the dark would come to light one day, but she never prepared for it to be that way. The fact that Royce and Lucky worked together made it even worse. Angel realized that it all could have gone bad a lot sooner.

Since Royce knew the truth, Angel's distress was raising the baby without him. The man she loved. She decided to still follow through with moving and getting the divorce even if she and Royce decided not to be a part of their child's life. She hoped that she could eventually get Royce to understand the reason behind her actions, so he could be in their child's life, and possibly give her another chance.

Angel pulled her car into the garage, parked, and got out. She walked into the house and heard Lucky in the exercise room. She was surprised that he was in there. He never went into their work out room.

"Hey baby!" he called out.

"Hey." she called back.

"Look in the kitchen on the table. I got you something." he said.

Angel rolled her eyes. He hadn't been that nice in years. At that point, it didn't matter what he did, she didn't like him anymore. There was nothing that he could do to make her want to be with him again. The marriage was over in her mind, with or without Royce.

"I hope my realtor calls me back soon about the house I want." she thought.

Angel walked into the kitchen and saw a box on the table. She opened it. There was an expensive pair of shoes inside. For someone who had been cheating on her for years, he still knew her style. She pulled the pretty heels out of the box and looked at them.

"They're nice, right?" Clarence asked from behind her. He wrapped his arms around her waist and kissed her on the shoulder.

"Yes, they are. Thank you." Angel said.

"I saw them, and I knew that you would like them."

"I do." she said.

"Babe look at me." he said, and then Angel turned to face him.

"When are you going to let me back in? I've been doing everything I am supposed to do. I miss my wife. When are you going to forgive me?"

"I'm sorry Lucky. It's just been busy at work and I am exhausted. Thanks for the shoes but can we talk about this another time? I need some sleep. Tomorrow is going to be another busy day."

Lucky sighed loudly, and then he nodded his head and said, "Ok. I understand."

He stepped back, so she could take the shoes with her upstairs to their room. She took a shower, and then she laid in bed and thought about Royce until she fell asleep.

Nia Rich

Clarence

&

Angel

Chapter 9

Clarence

Something was going on with his wife. Clarence could feel it. She had never stayed mad at him that long. A week maybe, but it had been a year. He knew that he didn't do right by Angel. He hadn't been doing right by her for years, but he wanted to show Angel that he was ready to make a change. Something about hearing her say that she didn't want to be with him anymore hurt his heart. He'd never considered his life without Angel in it. He'd basically raised her. Clarence had been with her since she was young, and they'd been through hell and back together. From her parents not approving of him, to being broke, and then building a life together.

Clarence loved Angel, but he grew bored with her, and that is why he started cheating. He got tired of their everyday routine. Even sex with her started to be monotonous to him. There was never any variety in their lives, and when Clarence tried to introduce Angel to something different, she wasn't interested. Angel buried herself in work. Clarence respected her drive, but she'd forgotten about taking care of him at home. Angel started treating sex with him like it was a chore. While Angel was doing that, other women were throwing themselves at him, so he got caught up in the attention that he was getting. Once he started cheating, he couldn't stop. Now, their marriage was in shambles over his mess. Angel had always forgiven him for his mistakes, but that time around was different. A knock at the door broke his thoughts.

Clarence said, "Come in."

Royce peeked his head into Clarence's office and said, "Hey Clarence, we have a meeting in five minutes."

"Alright." Clarence said.

He stood up and started gathering his folders and paperwork for the meeting. Clarence followed Royce out of his office. Royce was quieter than usual. As they walked towards the conference room for the meeting, he noticed that Royce wasn't talking to his at all. Clarence knew that Royce wasn't extremely talkative, but he would usually spark up small talk. Something was different about his energy, and Clarence could feel it. Clarence decided to break the awkward silence and sparked up some conversation.

"You alright today brotha?" Clarence asked.

"Yea. I 'm cool man. Why do you ask?"

"I don't know. You don't seem like yourself lately."

"Yea I am a little tired is all."

"I hear you. You left out of the party so fast the other night that you didn't get to see my team whoop your team's ass."

"Aw man stop it. That game was bullshit. Your team won by pure luck."

"Haha! You know my team killed your team, and you still owe me fifty bucks brotha."

"Aight. I got you." Royce said right before they walked into the large conference room full of top executives.

"Good morning." Clarence said when they walked in. After everyone greeted them, the two men sat down and started the meeting.

***

Angel was standing in the kitchen on her phone when Clarence walked in the house. She hung up when she saw him and put her phone into her pocket. Clarence walked up to her and kissed her on the cheek.

"Stop Lucky," she said as she pushed him away.

"Why?" he asked, and then he grabbed her around her waist and pulled her to him.

"I'm not in the mood for all that Lucky." she said as she pushed his arms from around her waist.

Everyone in Clarence's family called him Lucky. His professional acquaintances called him by his first name, Clarence. Lucky was the nickname his grandmother gave him because she said that he was always lucky. She gave him that nickname after he found a hundred-dollar bill on the ground while walking to school one day. His grandmother said that he would be blessed with fortune. When Clarence looked at his life, he always felt that his grandmother was right. He and his wife didn't want for nothing. He appreciated his grandmother for speaking his blessings into existence.

"I'm not trying to hear that baby. You are my wife now stop playing." Clarence said as he pulled her to him again.

"Would you stop?" she snapped.

"What is your problem Angel?"

"Nothing."

"I'm tired of you pushing me away."

"I don't feel like being bothered. I had a long day." she said.

"You don't think that I had a long day?" he asked.

"I'm sure you did."

"That's why I'm trying to get some loving from my wife."

"Well, I am not in a loving mood."

"You haven't been in a loving mood for a while now."

"And who's fault is that?"

"Are you're going to keep holding my mistakes against me? The night I came home late was a long time ago, and I have been doing everything right since then."

"You don't get to pick and choose when you want to act right and when I decide to forgive you."

"Come on Angel. We've been married for going on eleven years. You've never been mad this long."

"I don't want to talk about this right now."

"We need to talk because I need to know what is going on with you."

"Nothing is going on with me, so leave me alone."

"That's a damn lie Angel, and you know it. You've been staying up extra late and sleeping in the guest bedroom the last few nights, so don't stand here and tell me there is nothing going on. It's been months since I've made love to you. You won't talk to me. You're distant most of the time. I've been trying to make things right, and you're not letting me in."

"You want to know what's wrong!? You're never going to change! How many times have we been here, and you still go back to cheating on me!? I am tired of this! I don't want to do it anymore! I want a divorce!" she yelled.

The infamous D word flew out of her mouth so fast she didn't have time to catch it. It hit Clarence in the face like a good right hook. He never thought he would hear that come from her mouth. Clarence was silent for a moment trying to process what she said to him. He felt like his heart had dropped out of his chest. Clarence was at a loss for words.

"A divorce?" is all he could manage to ask.

"Yes." Angel said. She looked down at the ground, and then Clarence looked up at the ceiling.

He asked, "So, are you saying that you don't love me anymore?"

"I'm not saying that." Angel said while staring at the kitchen floor.

Clarence looked at her and asked, "So, what are you saying? You're willing to throw away almost eleven years and everything that we built together?"

Angel finally looked up from the floor, gave Clarence eye contact and said, "I'm saying that I am no longer happy in this marriage with you and there is no reason to keep trying to salvage something that is broken. You didn't care about our eleven years together when you were running around with all those hoes. You didn't care about our eleven years when I was sitting up late nights wondering where you were. Now suddenly, our eleven-year marriage is important to you."

Clarence stepped closer to her and said, "Baby. I love you."

"I don't want to hear it Lucky." Angel replied.

"Baby."

"Now you know where my mind is. There is nothing else to say."

"Baby I can make this right."

Angel shook her head and said, "No, you can't."

"What about our house? And everything else?"

"At this point, it doesn't matter to me."

"I'm not trying to hear that shit Angel, you're just tripping right now. We're in the heat of the moment and you're just talking out the side of your neck. I'm gonna give you some time to think about it."

"Don't need any time."

Clarence put his hand under her chin, pulled her face closer to his, and said, "I love you, you love me, and we are going to make it work. Period."

Chapter 10

Angel

Angel rolled her eyes and left Lucky standing in the kitchen. She didn't want to hear anything that he was saying. Angel's mind was already made up, but she was mad at herself for bringing up the divorce. Angel really didn't want to have that discussion until after she moved out, but Lucky was pushing the subject, and it slipped out. She felt that there was no need to keep stringing Lucky along. There was no chance to reconcile. She knew where her heart was. Angel didn't want Lucky to touch her, kiss her, or even try to have sex with her anymore. She didn't care to hear him say that he loved her. Angel felt like she was just done, and the situation with Royce had her feeling emotionally exhausted.

Angel was just praying that her realtor would get back to her about one of the two houses' she'd made offers for. Now that the cat was half way out of the bag, she needed to make moves fast. Angel didn't want to stick around any longer. She'd even given staying in a hotel for a while some thought.

Angel sent a text message to Tanisha as she made her way back through her large living room with the lofty ceilings towards the garage door. Angel asked Tanisha if she could stop by for a little bit. She needed to get out of the house and away from Lucky. She wasn't in the mood for him to keep trying to talk to be about her decision. Plus, she wanted to get somewhere that she can call Royce a dozen more times with hopes that he would finally answer the phone and talk to her. Tanisha text back telling Angel to stop over. Angel picked her purse up off one of the glass tables, and then she unlocked the garage door. Lucky heard her unlock the garage door and he hurriedly walked to where she was standing.

"Where are you going?" he asked when he turned the corner.

"To Tanisha's." Angel said.

"For what?" he asked.

"Does it matter?"

"Yes, it does."

"Because I want to."

"You've never went over there this time of night before."

"Well, I'm going now. I will see you later."

"We need to talk some more."

"About what, Lucky?"

"About our marriage."

"We've already done that."

"And nothing was resolved."

"Yes, it was."

"Getting a divorce is not a resolution Angel."

"Trying to hold on to something that is no longer there isn't either."

"That is a cop out."

"No, it's not. It's me saying I'm tired and I'm done."

"Something is not right. There is more to this than what you are telling me."

"Why does there have to be something more? It's simple. I think that I was clear. Now, you can do you and I don't have to stress about it."

"Baby." he said as he walked towards her, but she stepped back.

He said, "Don't you know how much I love you?"

"Um hum." she responded coldly.

"I'm serious."

"Um hum. I gotta go."

Angel turned on her heels and opened the door to the garage. She could still hear Lucky pleading his case over the sound of the garage door going up. Angel blocked him out, got into her car, and pulled out of the garage. She called Royce a couple of times on her way to Tanisha's house, but he didn't answer. Part of her still had hope because he hadn't blocked her number yet.

***

"What are you doing out this late?" Tanisha asked when she answered the door.

Angel laughed and said, "It's only nine o'clock."

"Yea and that's past your bedtime."

Angel laughed again before saying, "Oh hush. Lucky was getting on my nerves, so I left." Angel walked in and sat down on Tanisha's couch.

Tanisha followed her after closing the door. She sat down next to Angel and asked, "What happened?"

"Long story short; I told him that I want a divorce."

"What!? No way."

"Yes."

"I thought you said that you were going to wait?"

"I was, but we were having a heated conversation, I got caught up in the moment, and it slipped."

"Oh boy."

"I know. He started saying what he said before. That he wants to fix it. We can work it out. Blah, blah, blah. Like where was all that before we got to this point?"

"Right," Tanisha said, and then Angel's phone rang. She ignored Lucky's call.

"Lucky?" Tanisha asked.

"Yes."

Tanisha shook her head, and then she asked, "Did you tell him about the house too?"

"Hell no."

"Good."

"I don't need him trying to come around. Especially after I have this baby."

"About that. How are you feeling?"

"I'm fine."

"You're not showing yet."

"I know. I hope this lady gets back to me about this house soon. I've already been considering other options."

"You could always live here for a little while until you get situated. I know I don't have much, but you can have my couch."

"Thanks girl."

"I'm thinking about renting an apartment for a brief time, or staying in a hotel, if I don't hear from her in a couple of days."

"The apartment is a clever idea, but don't waste your money on a hotel when you can just stay here." Tanisha stood up and asked, "Are you hungry or thirsty? Would you like some water?"

"I'm not hungry, but I'll take some water."

Tanisha opened her refrigerator and pulled out two bottles of water. Angel ignored another call from Lucky, but he called right back, so she answered the phone.

"What Lucky?"

"I just wanted to make sure that you made it over there okay."

"I'm fine."

"Are you sure babe?"

"Yes."

"I've just never seen you act like this."

"I just need some time to think Lucky."

He exhaled loudly, and then there was a pause before he said, "Alright."

"I'll talk to you later." Angel said. She took the bottle of water from Tanisha's hand, and then Tanisha sat back down on the couch next to her.

Lucky said, "No matter what you think, I do love you."

"Ok."

"You don't love me anymore?"

"I didn't say that."

"Alright. Have fun."

"Bye." Angel hung up.

Tanisha said, "Damn Lucky has never been like that."

"I know."

"Maybe reality has finally hit him like a ton of bricks now that he realizes that he is not going to have you anymore."

"I think so." Angel said as she placed another call to Royce, but no answer.

"Have you talked to Royce yet?"

"Nope."

"Dang."

"I know. I've been thinking about just showing up to his house and forcing him to talk to me."

Tanisha laughed. "About to get gangster huh?" she asked.

Angel laughed too, and then she said, "Yes. It's the only way I am going to get him to talk to me. He can ignore my calls a million times, but how is he going to ignore me if I am in his face?"

"You've got a point, but what if he still won't talk to you?"

"Well, I'll take my loss and live with it, but I got to at least try one more time. I need him to know all the truth, so he will know that I'm not the dirty bitch he thinks that I am. I'm really in love with him, and I regret the way I handled everything."

"You know that I'm team Royce, so you got to do what you got to do. Just be careful."

"I will."

Clarence

Chapter 11

Clarence

Angel didn't make it home until after midnight, and then she went straight to their guest bedroom. Clarence noticed that she'd moved some of her clothes from their bedroom down there. He couldn't believe what was happening. Clarence was heated, but he stayed upstairs in their bedroom in his thoughts about everything.

For the first time, he felt remorseful for all the things that he had done during their marriage. He'd always given his wife an apology, but he never really meant it. Most of the time he was just saying it, so she would stop tripping. Clarence always knew that he was going to do it again. He'd be calling one of his other women shortly after apologizing, and then he would be having sex with one of them the next day, if not the same night. Out of all the times had pissed his wife off and apologized, Angel had never been as cold as she was that night. Clarence never thought he would see the day that they would be sleeping in separate rooms, or Angel would be asking for a divorce.

Clarence couldn't help but to keep thinking that something didn't feel right about it all. He kept feeling like there was more going on than her being pissed at him for coming home late the last time. Something about Angel was different. Besides her being cold and angry, he felt something had changed, and he couldn't put his finger on it, but he planned to find out.

Clarence quietly slid out of bed and walked down their winding staircase to the first floor. He walked down the hall and opened the door to the guest room. Clarence stood there for a while watching his wife sleep. She looked so beautiful, so angelic, and so peaceful. He watched how her chest rose and fell, and he listened to her light snores. Clarence loved sleeping next to her. He missed the warmth of her body next to him. It always made him feel at ease. Sometimes she was too warm, and he had turn up the air conditioner just to sleep next to her comfortably without sweating, but he was alright with that. Eleven years with her, and he was about to lose her over his foolishness. Clarence couldn't let that happen. He wanted to crawl in bed with her, but he decided to leave her be. He would try to talk to her again the next morning.

Chapter 12

Clarence

Clarence was sitting back thinking about the day that he met Angel. He remembered it like it was yesterday. He was just getting off work on a Friday. He was going to the bank to cash his check. Clarence was dog tired and ready to get home to relax. It was extremely hot outside and the news was warning people to stay hydrated and somewhere cool. The heat index was above one hundred and fifteen degrees and was going to be that way the rest of the week. Clarence pulled into the bank parking lot, and parked. As soon as he turned his car off, he could feel the heat from the sun cooking the earth through his tinted car windows.

He stepped out of the car into the dry desert heat. Clarence felt like he'd stepped into an oven and was being cooked like a rotisserie chicken. He walked quickly from his car into the bank as the sun broiled his back. Clarence was greeted by one of the bankers and offered a bottle of water. He accepted the offer and stepped into the line. That was when he noticed Angel. She was standing in the line one person in front of him. She had flawless brown skin, pretty lips, and soft features. Her soft black hair was in a ponytail, and he could tell that her hair was relaxed without any hair weave enhancements. Angel looked like she too was coming from work as she had a waitress apron tied around her waist. She wasn't wearing much make-up. She was gorgeous to him. Clarence tried to guess her age while he waited for the next teller. She looked young, but not too young. She didn't have the body of a little girl. She was fully developed. She had hips, breasts, and booty. Clarence guessed, that she was probably just turning twenty-one, which was still a little young for him being a fresh twenty-eight at the time, but he was still interested.

Clarence hoped that the teller he was working with would be quick as he wanted to try to talk to Angel before she left. When it was his turn to step up to the teller line, Angel looked over at him. They made eye contact, she smiled, and then turned back towards her teller who was counting her money. Clarence was happy that his teller was moving quickly. The one helping him was familiar with him. She cashed his check, deposited half of it, and counted the other half back to him in cash.

He took a swig from his bottle of water and kept an eye on Angel. He saw her pick up her money and start heading towards the door. Clarence put the cap back on his water, picked up his money, thanked the teller, and walked quickly towards the door. He caught her right when she was opening the second set of doors to go outside.

"Excuse me." Clarence said. His voice was deep and smooth. She turned to face him. Her eyes were slanted and seductive.

"Yes?" she asked.

"Um, Hi. You are so beautiful I just wanted to introduce myself."

"Oh. Thank you." she giggled. Her voice was soft and sweet. Not high pitched, but not deep. It was somewhere in between.

"I am Clarence, but people call me Lucky. What's your name?"

She said, "Angel." She smiled. Her teeth were perfect and white. Clarence extended his hand to shake hers. She shook his hand, and then moved out of the way so a few people could walk out of the bank.

"Nice to meet you Angel." Clarence said.

"Likewise." she responded.

"Looks like you're coming from work." he said.

"Yes, I am a waitress. I assume that you are doing the same?"

"Yes I am. I clean offices. I don't want to hold you up, but I would like to take you out sometime, if that is ok with you."

"Um, sure."

"Can we exchange numbers?"

"Sure." she said.

Clarence pulled out his yellow cell phone and slid the screen up. Angel pulled her pink flip phone out of her pocket. He dialed the number that she gave him into his phone and called hers. She said that she had it and would save it into her phone.

"Alright. I will be in touch soon Angel. It was nice to meet you."

"Nice to meet you too." She smiled again, and then the two of them walked back out into the Arizona desert heat. They walked past the palm trees decorating the banks entrance, and a couple of purple desert flower bushes, and then they said goodbye before getting into their cars. Clarence waved to her before he got into his. He was instantly agitated that his car my car felt like an oven set to three-hundred and seventy-five degrees. He quickly started it and turned on the air conditioning. Even with the tinted windows on his Honda Accord, the steering wheel felt hot to the touch. Clarence sat there for a few moments allowing his car to cool off, and then he pulled off.

Chapter 13

Clarence

They would end up going on a date a few days later. Clarence learned that Angel was a waitress at a restaurant in Phoenix, and she was a student in college studying dentistry. Angel told him that she had just turned twenty-one and was still living with her parents until she finished school. She also told him that she was driving her father's car until she saved enough to get her own.

Clarence told Angel how old he was, and that he lived alone in a one-bedroom apartment. He also told her that he too was in school trying to finish getting his degree. It had taken a while to buckle down and go to college, but once he figured out what he wanted to do, he was focused. Clarence told Angel that was the reason he had no kids, never been married, and was single. Angel told him that she was single too, and from that date forward, they were inseparable and on the fast track.

He found out that besides him, she had only been with one other guy that she dated in high school. To Clarence that meant Angel was practically a virgin. He wanted to do right by her, so he cut off every woman that was in his life at the time. Angel spent a lot of time at his apartment, and in four months they were engaged, and he was meeting her parents. That was when Clarence found out that Angel was younger than she said. Her father snapped about Clarence. After she introduced them, her father asked Clarence to step outside, so he could talk to Angel privately. Clarence listened to the argument from outside.

"You bring this grown man into my house! What does he want with you! You are a baby!" her dad yelled.

"No, I am not daddy! I am grown!"

"Eighteen years old is not grown and you think that you're mature enough to get married!? You can't even take care of yourself yet!"

When Clarence heard her dad say her true age, his eyes bulged.

"Calm down." Clarence heard her mother say.

"I will not calm down! You are my daughter and I am not ok with you dating a man that old! You are not grown! You are still a teenage little girl!"

"Daddy! I love him! I am not a little girl anymore! I am grown! You can't tell me what to do!"

"While you are living under my roof I can! You will end this relationship now!"

"I am not ending it!"

"Well you will get the hell up out of my house!"

"Mama!?"

"Baby please calm down." her mother said.

"Hell no!" her dad yelled.

"Fine! I'm gone!" Angel yelled.

"Angel! Don't you walk out of this house! If you walk out, don't come back!"

"I won't come back! Ever!"

Angel stormed out of the house and said, "Let's go."

Clarence followed Angel to his car as her mom held her dad back from storming out of the house to attack him.

"Stop it baby! Let her go! She will be back!" her mom yelled.

"Hell no! You damn Pedophile!" her dad yelled.

Angel and Clarence got into his car and drove off. She cried as they were driving. Clarence put his hand on her leg to try to calm her as they drove towards his house.

"Why didn't you tell me that you were only eighteen?" he asked.

"Because I wanted you to like me, and I didn't want you to look at me like a little girl. I wanted you to think that I was mature."

Clarence was silent. He didn't know what to do. Part of him felt like breaking up with her, but the other part felt like he had already had sex with her, fallen in love with her, and planned a life with her. Plus, her father had just kicked her out of the house. He couldn't just walk away from her, so he decided to stay with her and make it work.

"Look babe. I am upset, but I love you regardless, ok? I got your back. We will make it work." he said.

Chapter 14

Clarence

Clarence understood how her father felt from a man's point of view. He wouldn't have wanted young daughter messing with a grown ass man either, and had Clarence known her true age from the beginning, he would have backed all the way up. He respected everything Angel's parents were saying, but he promised Angel that he had her back, so he stood by his word.

In the beginning, things were hard for Clarence and Angel. Clarence was trying to get his life together at the time. He was driving a vehicle, but it wasn't a luxury car. Sometimes the air condition didn't work, and he was constantly fixing it. When Angel moved into his one-bedroom apartment, he didn't even have a full bed set. His mattresses were on a medal frame. He had one dresser and the rest of his clothes were either hung up or in storage tubs in his closet. Clarence had one television which was like one of the first flat screens ever built. It was a hand me down from a family member, and he accepted it with plans to get a new one. He had one couch, a coffee table, and a television stand all from Ikea. His dishes and appliances were all from Ikea as well. They had close to nothing, and it was a struggle, but they pushed forward with the marriage.

They got married at the court house with just his brother as a witness. His brother felt that Clarence was stupid as hell for marrying a girl so much younger than he was. He stood by his decision and did what he had to do. His wife was young, but she was mature, intelligent, ambitious, and she could cook. Everything he wanted in a woman, and all the things that he loved most about her. They made their home life work. Both worked hard to pay the bills and they both continued to go to school. They supported each other and helped each other work towards their goals.

Eventually, the arduous work paid off. Clarence graduated, and he went from cleaning the office to working in the office. Angel finished her bachelor's degree, and then she started working as a dental hygienist while still attending school to become a dentist. They went from sharing one car to having two, and then they moved from the one-bedroom apartment into a two-bedroom condo. Angel's parents had finally started to accept Clarence once they saw their growth and how much they held each other down.

Clarence and Angel were in love, focused, and moving full speed ahead. When Angel's father passed, it crushed her, but Clarence helped her through the pain. Angel pushed forward, graduated from dental school, and got her license. Clarence became a Marketing Manager, and then they traded in the cars they had for luxury vehicles. They moved from the condo into the big house, and then he helped her open her own dental office. Everything was good and getting better by the day.

Clarence's phone ringing broke his thoughts. He jerked out of his nostalgia and answered it.

"This is Clarence."

"Hey baby, can I come to the office and see you?"

"Not today. I have a lot going on."

"Aww. I miss you."

"I know, but I'll get back to you later ok?"

"Ok."

He hung up the phone and sat back in his office chair. He leaned back and looked up at the ceiling. The girl on the phone was one of the reasons why his marriage was ending. Not because his wife found out, but because of his carelessness. Clarence looked up at the ceiling and put his hands behind his head. As he stared up at the ceiling, thoughts of how his marriage started unraveling began to flood his mind.

Chapter 15

Clarence

Somewhere along the journey they lost their way. Somewhere along the way they got too busy for each other. They didn't talk as much, and they weren't hanging out anymore. At least that's the way it looked through Clarence's eyes. In the beginning, they were making love almost every day, but love making had starting to get sparse. Sometimes it felt to him felt like he was damn near begging for it.

Angel was always tired from work and school, and their schedules were opposite. Sometimes he would make it home and she would be studying until late. By the time, she made it to bed, Clarence would be sleep. Then, there were nights when he got home, she would already be sleep. He never wanted to disturb her, so he would leave her alone. That became their everyday routine, and when they did have sex, Clarence felt like she was only doing it to stop him from asking for it. The passionate part of their love making had dissipated and to Clarence it felt like *just sex*. Attractive women began showing him interest, and he started accepting it. He knew that most of the women were money hungry and materialistic. He knew they wanted him because of what they thought that he could do for them, but he enjoyed getting them to do things that his wife wasn't doing. Clarence relished the attention he was receiving. He understood their greed and played on it to get what he wanted. At first, he enjoyed it, but then he got carried away, and Angel found out.

Angel finding out was the reason the couple had no kids. Clarence and Angel discussed having children long before the infidelity started, and she told him that she didn't want to have kids. She told him that they worked too hard, and they wouldn't have time for them. Clarence disagreed. He wanted kids and he was not happy about her being against it, but Angel was adamant that she was unwilling to slow down to have children. After some years, Angel finally started talking about having a family, but she found out about the first girl Clarence was cheating on her with and changed her mind.

The first girl he cheated on her with he'd met online. It started with a few comments back and forth, and then it turned into full-blown conversations in instant messages. Next thing he knew, a few video chats had turned into him meeting her at her house, beating it up, and carrying on a sexual relationship for months. She was a beautiful woman, and she was a freak. Sometimes she would answer the door in lingerie when he would stop by her house. Clarence loved that as Angel never wore things like that. She always wore pajama sets to bed with her hair tied up in a scarf.

The affair was going well until the woman got in her feelings and got things twisted. She contacted Angel via social media, and it blew up in Clarence's face. He was in the dog house, but it only took a short while for Angel to forgive him. Angel started making love to him again, and things were back to normal for little while, but it didn't last long. In time, Clarence was back up to no good again.

He started hanging out with some of his guy friends and his brother a lot. One of the places they liked to hang out was at a strip club. He met a dancer there and started messing with her. He spent a lot of money on the young woman, and then he slipped up a couple of times and had unprotected sex with her. A pregnancy scare stopped him in his tracks. He knew that he was tripping. He wanted a baby, but not with an exotic dancer.

The young woman was sexy as hell, and she would keep him out late nights. She would give him head in the car, swallow, and she loved to ride him. Clarence and the dancer never had sex indoors. Always in his car on some dark street. That is what he liked about her. Angel never wanted to do sexual things outside of the house with Clarence. Angel barely liked to do anything sexual outside of the bedroom.

Clarence messing with the exotic dancer caused a lot of arguments, and he had to come up with a lot of lies to cover up what he was doing. Angel was never able to prove it, but she speculated, and she was not quiet about it. She constantly questioned him and accused him of doing things behind her back, but she never had solid evidence to back up what she was fussing about. Clarence would just tell her that she was tripping or acting crazy. He was thankful the stripper didn't end up being pregnant, so he ended the relationship. The arguing stopped after he ended it with that girl and everything was good for a while. Until he started messing with the girl at work.

Margo was thick in all the right places. She had a pretty face, a slim waist, thick thighs, and a voluptuous bottom. She loved wearing pencil skirts, tight fitted pants, and pretty blouses that accentuated all her curves. Clarence had a thing for lips and hips, and she had both. She had sex appeal and she wanted him. He tried to ignore her advances, but his flesh got the best of him. He gave into temptation and started having an affair with her shortly after she began working for the company.

Margo's favorite thing was to give him head in his office or have him meet her on the first level of the building in a private bathroom to have sex. It was fun until Clarence saw her flirting with Royce one day. He checked her, and then he fell back on her for a little while. Up until the night he was out late before Angel went on the cruise with her friends. Clarence told himself after that night that he needed to chill. Especially when he saw how cold Angel was to him the next day. When she returned from the cruise with that same cold attitude, he knew that he had messed up big time.

Clarence was in panic mode since that night trying to fix his mistakes. He knew that he had messed up big that time. He was so caught up in his world thinking that he had it, feeling like the big man on campus, and thinking that she would never be done with him. Clarence was practically her first everything. First real sexual experience, first real love, first real relationship, and first marriage. In his mind, she was never going anywhere, and then she hit him with the D word. It blew his mind. He knew then that Angel was fed up and wanted to leave. He was having a tough time grasping that fact. Clarence knew she was angry with him, but divorce was extreme in his mind.

He felt like there was something or someone else helping her to make that decision. Something or someone else was trying to pull his Angel away from him, and he couldn't let that happen.

Royce

Chapter 16

Royce

I knew that I wasn't myself. I didn't feel like myself since finding out about Angel and Clarence. Clarence of all people. My boss. I had to look at her husband's face every day at work. The whole situation had drained me mentally and physically. There I was trying to marry someone else's wife unknowingly.

I was duped by a woman who had me thinking that we were in this together. Angel's clever ass played the hell out of me. I never knew that a woman could be so slick and conniving. She had me looking like a sucker. I introduced her to my family, bought her a ring, gave her the key to my house, and it was all bullshit.

She knew that she was married to someone else the entire time. Not even separated, but married, and living together. I couldn't erase it from my mind. She knew she was up to no good, and I was the fool all wrapped up in it. I was fuming, and I wished that I had never met her. I regretted the day that I ran into her in the store. If I could've taken that day back, I would've.

I felt stupid for trying to marry my high school crush. I didn't know what the hell I was thinking. I never gave my heart to a woman, and the one time I do, I get played. It didn't make it any better that I had to see the fool she was married to everyday. I couldn't stand seeing Clarence, and I thought about looking for work elsewhere, but that meant giving up on my promotion and my raise over the mess. I was not willing to mess up my money for some bullshit, so I decided to try to erase it all from my mind. I figured erasing her would be the best way to get over it.

"Where are you at man?" Greg asked.

I guess I was standing there in a daze for a moment. I had zoned out of the conversation they were having and into my thoughts about Angel.

"Yea. Is everything ok bro?" Darnell asked.

"Yea. I'm good." I said.

"You don't seem like yourself." Kevin said.

"I just got a lot on my mind." I said.

"It ain't 'ole girl is it?" Greg asked.

"Naw we cool. Just work stressing me. Got a lot of projects and stuff piling up." I lied.

"Ah yea. Well, you got that promotion, so you know what they say, more money more problems." Kevin said.

"They gonna work you like a slave for that extra money too." Darnell said.

I pepped up, changed the subject, and said, "Absolutely, so bro, I see you and your baby momma are back on good terms."

"Yea bro, she let a brother come back home. You know how it is. She was missing this dick. She can't stay away from that too long."

"I know that's right bruh, bruh." Greg said as he slapped hands Darnell.

"Hopefully this time you'll do right, so she ain't throwing your shit on the lawn." I said.

The guys laughed, and then Greg asked, "Wait, what?"

"Yea man, socks, draws, and all." I said while they continued to laugh.

Darnell said, "You just gonna put my shit out there, bro? Aight."

"I didn't put it out there. Your girl put it out there in front of the whole neighborhood. For all to see."

Greg and Kevin continued to laugh, and then I said, "I had to rescue this fool like I was animal rescue coming to save an abused dog."

"Nah bruh." Greg said in between laughs.

"Yea, she was bopping him upside the head 'n shit." I said, and then I laughed with Greg and Kevin.

"Aight." Darnell said through laughs. "That's enough."

"Aight. I just hope you learned your lesson little bro." I said.

Greg said, "Yea. What happened to relationship goals? That don't sound like relationship goals to me."

"Ah man. Y'all gonna get up off me." Darnell said through laughs.

We laughed a little longer, and then we talked about the Trump and Clinton presidential election. We debated politics for a while, and then Greg told us one of his colorful stories about some new chick he was messing with. After another beer and another game, I left and headed home.

When I got into my Camaro, I checked my phone. I had four missed calls from Angel and a text from this chick I met at Quick Trip gas station. I didn't know why I gave her my number. I called myself getting over Angel. The girl wasn't even that appealing to me, but she was giving me the eyes. I was just doing something to make myself feel better. I ignored the text, and then my phone rang, so I answered it.

"Sup?"

"What's up stranger?"

It was Shelly. I hadn't talked to her in a long time. I was surprised she still had my number.

"Nothing much. Same 'ole stuff, different day. What's up with you?"

"I haven't talked to you in a while and I wanted to see how you were doing." she said.

"Yea. I'm surprised to hear from you. It's been a while."

"Are you, busy tonight?" she asked.

I thought about it for a second, and then I said, "No, I'm not busy."

"I miss you and I would like to see you, if that's possible."

"Yea come through. I should be home soon."

"Ok. I'll be over in thirty minutes. See you later."

I disconnected the call and smiled. It was exactly what I needed. A fat ass and some good pussy to get over Angel. Shelly's random call was right on time.

***

Shelly was looking better than the last time I saw her. It looked like she had been working out a lot. Her six - pack was harder than mine.

"Damn girl, you've been hitting the iron hard, haven't you?" I playfully asked as I eyeballed her body in the coral, two-piece, crop top and skirt set she had on. Her booty looked even fatter than before.

"Yea that and waist training," she said with a smile.

"I see," I said as I reached out to hug her.

Her brown skin was soft and smelled like a sweet mixture of vanilla and coconut. Most times my manhood would be moving at the sight of her, but it wasn't moving. All that soft ass in front of me and my manhood wasn't responding. I shut the door telling myself that it was early enough in the evening to smash her, get her to leave, and watch a television movie that I recorded, before going to bed.

I asked, "Would you like some water or something else to drink?"

"Do you have some alcohol?"

"Light or dark?"

"Dark."

"Hennessey?"

"Yea that's fine."

"Ice?"

"Yes."

"Alright."

I think she could sense something different because I wasn't all over her like I was before. I let her lead me to my kitchen, so I could watch her ass bounce in the jersey knit skirt she had on. Shelly was a chocolate fox, but my manhood still wasn't moving. I put ice in a glass, poured a shot over the ice, and then I poured a little dark soda into the glass. I made a drink for myself, handed her the glass, and she followed me down the short flight of steps to my den.

We sat down on my leather couch. She gave me a seductive look before drinking a little of the alcoholic beverage. There was an awkward silence. The kind when neither person knows what to say because they really don't know each other outside of the bedroom.

She broke the silence by asking, "How have you been?"

"I've been alright." I responded.

"You look good."

"So, do you." Shelly said, and then she smiled and gulped down the remainder of the drink. She put the glass on the table next to her.

"Well I've missed you." she said.

She leaned forward and kissed my neck a few times, and then she kissed my ear softly and seductively while rubbing the crotch area of my black sweatpants. My manhood still wasn't moving, so I closed my eyes to try to get into the moment. She reached down into my sweatpants and touched my manhood. I was soft. *Damn.* I thought, *"What is wrong with me?"*

I started trying to concentrate to help the situation, but still no response. Shelly pulled my manhood out while soft. I guess she figured that she would suck me into an erection. Shelly laid down on her stomach and put my soft squishy flesh into her mouth. I put my hand on her soft ass. I figured rubbing on the softness would get me aroused. Nothing. Shelly noticed. She stopped sucking.

She asked, "What's wrong?"

"I don't know." I said.

"You've never been like this before."

"I know. I'm sorry Shelly I just have a lot on my mind and I shouldn't have invited you over. It's not you. It's me." I said. She let go of my manhood and started to sit up.

"It's ok." she said., and then I apologized again while putting my manhood back inside of my boxer briefs and adjusting my sweatpants.

"Well, it's all good. I was just trying to get a little from you before I get married."

"Married?" When are you getting married?"

"Tomorrow. I just wanted to get some of that good dick before I take myself off the market."

She stood up and adjusted her skirt, and then she said, "I am going to go now. You take care." She started walking towards the door.

The hell? This chick got my D in her mouth the night before she is going to walk down the aisle and kiss some other dude and say I Do? I thought.

When I opened the door to let her out, Angel was standing there. It looked like she was about to ring my doorbell but stopped in her tracks when the door opened.

Shelly paused, and Angel frowned. For a second, I thought that it was going to be a scene like in the movie Friday when Nia Long's character walked out of Craig's house and Paula Jai Parker's character was standing on the porch.

Shelly looked back at me, smiled, and then she said, "Good night."

She walked past Angel and headed to her car. Angel stepped back and watched her walk away, and then she looked at me.

Chapter 17

Royce

"What are you doing here?" I asked with a frowned face.

Angel said, "I came to talk to you, but I guess I came at the wrong time." She did a hand gesture towards Shelly pulling away in her car.

"You shouldn't be showing up here unannounced, Angel." I said angrily.

"I need to talk to you, and you blocked my number."

"Because I don't want to talk to you, and you keep calling."

"It has been three weeks."

"And?"

"And we need to talk."

"Angel we've already talked, and I told you that I was through."

"So just like that?"

I shook my head and looked around my neighborhood. I didn't want my neighbors to be listening to our conversation through dark windows, so I told her to come inside. After I closed and locked the door, I turned to face her.

"What was that?" She made a hand gesture towards the door.

"What?"

"Three weeks and you've already moved on?"

"A married woman shouldn't have anything to say to me about who's in my house." I said coldly.

"Wow."

"Is exactly what I said when I found out about your secret marriage Angel."

"I came over here to talk to you about that."

I exhaled loudly and looked at the floor. I wasn't ready to see her.

"It's not what you think."

"I think you lied. Are we going to go through this again? Because I got stuff to do." I said.

Her eyes began to water and then she went into a long rant.

"Royce, I didn't mean to lie to you, ok? I'm sorry. I know I messed up in the beginning because I should have just told you, but I didn't think it was going to get deep. In the beginning, I was just doing it because I wanted to cheat back on my husband. I wanted to get him back for all the women he had slept around with while married to me. I was fed up, and you walked right into my misery. It felt good to cheat back, but when our feelings got involved, I started to feel bad about it all. I wasn't expecting for us to fall in love. Once I realized that it was happening, I wanted to tell you, but I didn't want to lose you. I wanted to divorce him way before you came into the picture. I just didn't want to fight. I regret that this all happened this way, but I am in love with you, and I want to be with you. I'm carrying your child not his. We can get a paternity test. I stopped sleeping with my husband when you came into the picture. The truth is, I was looking for that house, so I could file for divorce. I wanted to move before filing to avoid any conflict. That is everything. The whole truth."

She blurted all that out in what seemed like one breath. Like she only had ten seconds left on the time clock to say everything she needed to say. She wiped a tear, and I snapped.

"Angel that shit hurt me! Do you know how it feels to find out that you are the only dummy in the room!? The last one to know something important! Huh?"

"I know. Probably how I felt when I found out that my husband was cheating on me the first time." Angel said, and then she wiped a tear.

"You shouldn't have lied to me Angel!"

"I know Royce and I hate that I did! I'm sorry."

"Quit saying that shit."

"What am I supposed to say?"

"I don't know!"

"Royce."

"He is my boss!"

"I didn't know that!"

"I wish I never met you Angel! I wouldn't have to be going through this shit! Why me? Huh? Why put me in the middle of this bullshit!"

"I didn't mean for it to be like this!"

"You had plenty of time to tell me!"

"I didn't know how!"

"Man!" I grabbed the bridge of my nose with my finger and my thumb and then I turned away from her.

"I love you Royce."

I turned back towards her and asked, "Are you sure about that?"

"Yes!"

"You're not supposed to lie to the person that you love."

Angel stepped to me and touched me. "I will never lie to you again. I promise."

"Don't touch me Angel." I said as I moved her hands.

Angel said, "I want to make things right you."

"How the fuck am I supposed to trust you huh!? You had a whole life that I knew nothing about! That is some deceitful shit!"

"I know baby, but-"

"But what?"

"I'm having this baby. I don't want to be with him anymore. I'm still moving out and filing for divorce. I just hope that one day you will forgive me and be a part of our child's life."

I was still angry. I was silent. I didn't know what else to say.

"I got to go." she said.

"Going home to him, right?"

"It's not like that."

"Whatever."

Nia Rich

I walked her to the door and she left.

Chapter 18

Royce

I was in my backyard with my brother Darnell. We were grilling up some chicken and steaks and talking. It was a warm night, but not hot. He was standing next to me with a beer in his hand. We'd just finished talking about his baby's mother, and then he changed the subject.

"So, what's up bro? Talk to me because you know I wasn't believing nothing that you said when we were playing pool, so what's really up?"

I flipped the steaks, hung the silver, metal tongs on the handle, and then I pulled the top down over the grill. I picked up my beer and turned towards him.

I said, "You're right, bro."

"So, what's up?"

"It's Angel. She's married."

"What? You're shitting me." he said, and then he shook his head a few times.

"I wish I was."

"The fuck?"

"I know."

"How did you find out?"

"She showed up to the Super Bowl party with him and she didn't know that I was there."

"Damn. Bitches are scandalous."

"Yea."

"Did you talk to her about it?"

"Yea."

"What did she say?"

"That she had been unhappily married the whole time and planning to file for a divorce, but here is the kicker."

"What?"

"She is pregnant with my child."

"Get the fuck out of here!" he said.

I nodded my head.

"Yea."

"Damn bro you got a baby on the way and you didn't tell me!?"

"She didn't want me to tell anybody and now I understand why, so keep it to yourself for real. I don't want mom finding out until I figure everything out."

"I won't say shit, but are you sure that's not her husband's baby bro?"

"She says it's not."

"Get a paternity test."

"And you know this."

"That ain't the half though bro."

"What there's more? What, is she pregnant with twins?"

"Nah. Her husband is my boss."

"Oh, hell nah."

"Right."

"Did she know that?"

"No. She was just as shocked as I was when we saw each other at that party."

"Hell naw." my brother said. His eyebrows hadn't gone down since I dropped the bomb.

"I know bro." I shook my head.

"I guess congrats on the baby if it's yours." he said as he slapped hands with me.

"Thanks."

What are you gonna do?" he asked.

"I don't know. I would be lying if I said that I don't love her."

"Yea but you can't let some chick just play you."

"This is true."

Damn. I wasn't expecting for you to tell me anything like this."

"I know. I didn't foresee it either."

"I don't know if you plan on taking her back, but either way. I am here if you need me bro. For real."

"Thanks."

Royce

Angel

Clarence

Chapter 19

Angel

Angel and Royce didn't talk for another week, after the impromptu meeting and discussion at his house. Angel called him a couple of times, but he didn't answer, so she gave up. She got the house that she wanted at the price she wanted, so she moved forward with it, and prepared to move. She decided that it was time to talk to her mom about everything. Angel wasn't ready to tell her everything that is going on, but she didn't have much time left. Angel noticed that she'd gained a little weight, and she knew that her baby bump would star growing anytime. Her mom was about to find out once again that her Angel wasn't much of an angel.

Angel was at work trying to get through her morning when she got an unexpected text message from Royce.

R: Are you free at lunch time?

Angel smiled when she saw the text.

"What?" Tanisha asked.

"Royce just asked me, if I am free for lunch." Angel said.

Tanisha said, "I knew he would come around."

Angel smiled again and sent Royce a reply message.

A: Yes, I am free.

R: Meet me at my house at noon. I want to talk to you.

Angel looked at Tanisha and said, "He says he wants me to come by at noon, so he can talk to me."

"That is awesome!" Tanisha said. She walked over and hugged Angel.

Angel smiled and said, "I hope it goes well."

"It will girl. You don't have any clients this afternoon. You better go and get your man." Tanisha said.

***

Angel was sitting on the couch looking at Royce standing up against the wall. The way he is standing, she could see his side profile. He had one foot up against the wall, and he had his arms folded across his chest. He was dressed in a Kenneth Cole suit and tie. Royce's arms and chest were bulging like he had been working out more than usual. Of course, he was looking good to Angel, but she was anxious to hear what he wanted to say to her. He looked like he was trying to figure out what to say.

After a few moments of silence, Royce said, "I've thought about everything."

Angel said, "Ok."

"I have a question, and I want you to answer it truthfully." he said.

"Ok."

"Is that my baby?"

"Yes."

"You're one hundred percent sure?"

"I'm one thousand percent sure."

"And you are sure that you're ok with taking a paternity test."

"I wouldn't have it any other way. I want you to trust me again."

"Everything you told me about your marriage is true?"

"Absolutely."

"So, you haven't had sex with him?"

"No."

"Since when?"

"Since I started messing with you."

Royce inhaled, and then he exhaled loudly. He looked down at the ground, and then he looked back up at Angel.

He said, "I don't know why I believe you, but I do."

He walked over and sat down next to her on the couch.

He said, "This is all messed up."

"I know."

"But I love you."

"I love you too."

"Come here."

Angel slid closer to him. He put his hands on her face, pulled her to him, and kissed her.

"I missed you." Angel said.

"I missed you more." Royce replied.

He put his hand on her stomach and asked, "How is my baby doing?"

"Fine."

"I'm willing to work through this because I love you, and I want to be a part of my baby's life." he said.

"Thank you." Angel replied.

"It's going to be a challenge being that he is my boss, but we will make it work until your divorce goes through and I find other work."

"Ok."

"You can move in here with me, and since the house you bought is bigger than this one, we will move, and then we will rent this one. How does that sound?"

Angel smiled, and then she asked, "Does this mean that you forgive me?"

"It means that I am working on forgiving you, but I understand that people make mistakes. No one's perfect."

"Thank you."

"So, did you mess around?" she asked.

"I was going to, but I couldn't." he said, and then Angel nodded her head.

Royce said, "I see you took your wedding ring off."

"Yea. There is no need to wear it anymore."

"How did you end up marrying a fool like that anyway?"

Angel shook her head. "It's a long story. I was young. We fell in love fast, and we got married fast. We struggled but we grew and built a life together. My parents hated him at first."

"Yea. Isn't he a lot older than you?"

"Yes. Ten years. They were totally against our marriage, but I had to be grown. I had to prove them wrong."

"I ain't no hater, but that dude is no good. You deserve better than that. He doesn't respect you." Royce said.

"I know, and that's why I can't do it anymore. Honestly, I thought that I was gonna cheat back, feel better, and keep it moving. Immature, yes, but, it's my reality. I wasn't expecting this."

"I understand," he said and then he kissed her.

The feeling of his soft lips pressed against hers made her tingle. Angel put her hand on his pants and started rubbing his erection. Royce didn't waste any time removing her lab coat, her shirt, and taking her breast into his mouth. Angel unbuckled his belt, unbuttoned his pants, and unbuttoned his shirt. Royce removed them and his boxer briefs, and then Angel took him into her mouth. Royce whispered her name a few times, and then he stopped her. He removed the rest of his clothing, kissed her stomach, and then he began kissing her peach. He gently flicked his tongue on her pearl and made her moan. Angel said his name repeatedly until she had an orgasm.

After she finished shivering, Royce said, "Let's go upstairs."

He followed Angel up the stairs to his bedroom. He laid down on his bed and told her to come to him. She knew that meant he wanted her to sit it on his taste buds. She crawled up his body and put her peach on lips again. She heard him moan, and then she fell into a zone. Angel held on to the head board as she rocked on his tongue. Royce held on to her backside as she moaned to the ceiling, said his name again, called for God, and told him that he was going to make her cum. Angel squeezed the headboard as her orgasm paralyzed her once again. When she regained composure, she crawled back down his body and put his erection inside of her. She bounced on it, grinded on it, turned around to face the other way on it, bounced on it some more with her breasts on his legs and his hands on her butt. Angel told him that she was going to orgasm again, and after she did, she got off it and took it into her mouth. She sucked her juices off his manhood while he watched her with much desire in his eyes.

When he felt himself close to an orgasm, he stopped her and put her on her back. He spread her legs as wide as they could go and put his mouth on her peach again. He licked her pearl again for a while before putting himself back inside of her. Royce kept her legs spread open in airplane position while he pounded into her. Angel moaned, Royce moaned, he grunted, she said his name, he said her name, he told her that he loved her, and she replied the same. Angel wiped sweat from Royce's forehead as he continued to make love to her. She felt him swell inside of her right before he was about to lose it. He told her that he was going to cum, and then he released himself inside of her. Royce kissed Angel passionately before lying next to her in the bed.

He said, "Damn I missed you."

"I missed you too." she said.

"I wish I didn't have to go back to work." Royce said.

"Me too." Angel said before sitting up and getting out of bed.

She walked downstairs to get her purse from the couch. Angel took her phone out of her purse and saw that she had about twenty missed calls from Lucky and Tanisha. She also received a bunch of text messages from Lucky asking her where she was, and Tanisha telling her to call her right away.

"Oh shoot, what is going on?" Angel said out loud.

"What's wrong?" Royce asked.

"I don't know. Lucky and Tanisha have been blowing my phone up."

"Lucky?"

"Yea. Well, you know him as Clarence. I got to get dressed and go." Angel said. She called Tanisha on her way to the bathroom.

"Hey girl. What's wrong?" she asked when Tanisha answered.

"Girl Lucky is up here looking for you. He says he is going to wait here for you to come back. He has been here for about forty-five minutes. Dang girl you been gone longer than an hour. I ran out of excuses for you."

"What the hell is he doing there?" Angel asked.

"I don't know. He showed up right after you left."

"I'm sorry. I didn't mean to be gone this long. I am heading back now." Angel said.

"Ok." Tanisha said, and then they hung up.

Angel hurriedly took a shower, redressed, reapplied make-up, and left Royce's house.

Chapter 20

Clarence

Clarence was for sure something was up with his wife. He'd been sitting at her office for over an hour waiting for her to make it back from where ever she was. Tanisha told him that she was at the bank, but he knew that it didn't take an hour to make a bank run. Plus, he'd called her several times, and she didn't answer. Clarence was getting increasingly irritated as time continued to go by with no word from Angel.

Clarence was at work when he decided to pop up on her for a spur-of-the-moment lunch date. He knew that there was a possibility that she wouldn't be able to go, but he thought it would make her happy to see him trying, and maybe change her mind about the divorce. After Clarence finished looking through his social media timeline, he put his phone back into his pocket and picked up one of the dental magazines.

"Hi Mr. Johnson. How are you?" One of Angel's dental assistants said to him when they walked in.

"Hi. It's good to see you." he replied.

"You too." she said as she continued to walk towards the back. Angel walked in shortly after her.

"Hey, what are you doing here?" she asked when she walked in. She gave Clarence a fake hug because she knew her employees were watching.

"I came to see you." Clarence said.

"Oh. You didn't tell me that you were coming." Angel replied.

"I know. I wanted to surprise you." Clarence said. He noticed that her body language was different, and she looked like she was nervous.

"Oh, alright." she said.

"Can we go outside and talk?" Clarence asked.

"Let me see if I have any appointments."

"Shouldn't you know that?"

"Yea, but I just want to double check."

Angel walked over to her receptionist and asked if she had any appointments. The receptionist shook her head back and forth, so Angel turned and walked back over to Clarence.

"I'm ready." she said.

"Ladies first." Clarence said. He followed her to the door, and then he held the door open, so she could walk out. He followed Angel to his car, and then they got in. Clarence turned the car on, and then he turned on the air conditioner.

He asked, "Where were you?"

"I was running some errands." Angel lied.

"Running errands takes you that long?" Clarence asked.

"Why does it matter how long it takes me? I had stuff to do." Angel said.

"Like what?"

"Really Lucky?"

"What do you mean really?"

"Are you really asking me for a run-down of everything I had to do?"

"Yea."

"I'm not doing that."

"Why not?"

"Because it's ridiculous."

"What is ridiculous about me asking my wife why she is not at work when I show up to surprise her?"

"I had stuff to do."

"It's not like you to disappear, and then not answer your phone when both Tanisha and I are calling you."

"I didn't hear my phone."

"You never keep your phone on silent."

"Well, it was today."

"Why?"

"I don't know."

"That's bullshit Angel and you know it."

"No, it's not. I didn't realize that it was on silent until I was on my way back."

"You have a business to run. People need to get in contact with you always. Why would you not notice that your phone is on silent?"

"Look, I don't have to argue with you about this."

"You are my wife, and I want to know where you've been Angel." Clarence said angrily.

"I just told you."

"No, what you told me was some bullshit!" he yelled.

"Lucky, I am not about to do this with you in front of my business."

"So, it doesn't matter to you that I came here to take you to lunch."

"I didn't say that."

"Your actions say it."

Angel rolled her eyes at Clarence and looked out of the window. She watched a few people walk past the palm trees in front of her business and into the optical store next door.

"It's clear that you don't give a fuck about my feelings."

"Did you care about my feelings when you were running around with all those whores you've been with?"

"Why are you bringing up old shit?"

"It might be old to you, but it's fresh to me."

Clarence said, "You can't even look me in my eyes. Look at me."

"For what?"

"Because I am talking to you." Angel slowly turned her head from the window and looked at Clarence.

"Is there someone else?" he asked.

"What?" she asked.

"Are you giving yourself to someone else?"

"Haven't we already had this conversation?"

"I need to know."

"No, Lucky." she said.

Clarence saw it in her eyes when she said it. She was lying to him. She didn't love him anymore and he could feel it. Clarence's body started to heat up from anger. Angel turned her head and looked out the window again.

"Do you love me anymore?" he asked.

"You've already asked me that."

"Tell me." he said, but Angel was silent.

"Tell me Angel! Do you love me anymore!?"

She looked back at him with tears in her eyes and said, "No, I don't."

Clarence's heart crushed, a headache formed in the back of his head, and he felt weak. He never thought he would hear those words from his wife's mouth. Hearing her say she wanted a divorce was one thing, but Angel telling him that she didn't love him anymore was like she stabbed a knife into his heart.

"That's messed up Angel. I would never say that to you. I would never stop loving you no matter what we go through."

"You stopped loving me, when you started cheating on me."

"Is that why you're cheating on me?"

"I don't know what you're talking about."

"You know what I'm talking about."

"Lucky, thank you for coming to take me out to lunch, but my client just walked in, so I have to go."

Clarence watched Angel get out of his car and walk back into her work place, and then he pulled out of the parking spot and drove away.

***

When Clarence made it back to work, he sent a text message to Margo and told her to stay back after everyone left so, she could bless him with her lips and mouth. Margo did what he asked. After the last person left the office, Margo walked into his office wearing an A-line dress that showed off her legs. Her peanut butter complexion and her sexy walk turned him on immediately. Margo got straight to business. She locked the door, walked over to him, dropped to her knees and started unbuckling his belt.

"I missed you daddy," she said before putting his hard, brown, flesh into her mouth. She wasn't playing any games with it. She used both hands as she bobbed her head up and down. She kept her rhythm steady as she went to work on him. Clarence tilted his head back in his office chair, closed his eyes, blocked out thoughts of Angel's lies, and let Margo handle her business.

Chapter 21

Clarence

After Margo blessed Clarence with some of the best head known to man, he bent her over his desk and gave her peach the business. When they were finished, he asked to trade cars for a couple of hours. Margo jumped at the chance to drive his Mercedes Benz. She didn't ask any questions. He told her that he would meet her at her house to trade back later in the evening, and then he left work.

Clarence pulled into his neighborhood and parked Margo's car a few houses away from his house. He knew Angel was home because he could see that the lights were on. He sat and watched his house in silence. Eventually,

Angel exited their house dressed in something different from what she wore to work. She got into her car and pulled out. Clarence slid down in his seat and let her drive past him. He slid back up and let her get a block down before he started driving. He stayed one car behind her driving the entire way. He followed her until she turned onto a block with houses. Clarence kept going, so that she wouldn't be suspicious. He pulled onto another block and laid low for a while. When he felt the coast was clear, he drove down the block she turned on until he spotted her car. He saw it parked in the driveway of a two-story house with a cactus in front of it. Clarence didn't know who's house it was. He knew that Tanisha lived in an apartment complex, and Angel's mom lived in Phoenix. The house she was at was in Chandler, and the other car in the driveway looked familiar. Clarence parked a few houses down, turned off his lights, and put the seat back a little. Clarence decided to sit back and wait patiently for her to exit the house. While he was waiting, he kept trying to place where he'd seen the other car that was in the driveway. Clarence began scrolling through his social media timeline to keep him busy while he waited. Finally, after an hour and forty-five minutes, Angel emerged, and he couldn't believe his eyes when he saw the person she was hugging at the door.

Royce.

His co-worker, and his friend. Royce.

Clarence felt anger boiling up inside of him as he watched Angel hug and kiss the half-dressed man that Clarence saw every day at work. He watched Angel turn to walk to her car, and then smile and wave at Royce before pulling off. Clarence watched Royce wave back, and then close the door. Clarence sat there stewing in his anger thinking about kicking Royce's door in and beating him down right there.

This dirty mutha fucka has been fucking my wife behind my back and smiling in my face every day. I should beat his ass at work tomorrow in front of all the staff. Who the fuck does he think he is? How dare Angel fuck one of my friends? My subordinate. All up under my nose. The nerve of these two!

Clarence was beyond angry, but he decided to relax. He started the car and drove away.

Chapter 22

Royce

I was sitting in my office going through some paperwork when I heard a knock at the door.

"Come in!" I called out.

Margo opened the door and said, "Hi Royce."

"Hey Margo. How can I help you?" I asked.

"I was wondering if you could help me with this. Clarence is not in his office." Margo said. She lifted a file with papers in it to show me.

"Sure. Have a seat." I said.

"Thank you." she said.

She closed the door and sauntered all the way into my office swaying her wide hips with every step. She sat down in the chair in front of my desk and put the papers on my desk. She pointed her spiky, red, acrylic nail to the paper.

"This is what I am confused about."

I looked at the paper and begin to explain what she was confused about. I could feel her eyes on me instead of on the paper. Every time I would ask, "Do you understand?" She would look back at the paper and tell me that she understood. She was making me feel uncomfortable, but I continued to provide the help she asked for.

"I don't mean to be disrespectful, and I hope that you don't take this the wrong way, but you have very nice skin." she said.

"Thank you, Margo." I said, and then I went back to explaining the issue.

"You are a very handsome man, Royce." she touched my hand, and then I moved my hand nervously.

"I'm sorry to be so forward, but I want you, I've always wanted you. I feel like you've always wanted me too." she said, and then she stood up and walked around my desk.

"No. Margo what are you doing?" I asked.

She smiled at me seductively and tried to straddle me. I pushed her off me. I stood up and said, "Margo, you got to get out of here."

"Why?" Margo asked. She tried to wrap her arms around me, but I brushed them off me and stepped back.

"Stop. You got to go. Don't ever do this again." I said, and then I pointed towards the door.

"Ok. Suit yourself, but your missing out on the best pussy that you will ever have."

She turned on her heels, picked her papers up off my desk, and walked towards the door. I heard a knock on my door as Margo was on her way out. She opened the door and Clarence was standing there.

"Hey Margo." Clarence smiled at her.

"Hey Clarence. I was just looking for you. I need your assistance."

"Meet me in my office."

"Ok. Bye Royce. Thanks for the help." she said. She walked out. Clarence watched her walk out, and then he asked, "Did you help her?"

"Not the kind of help she was looking for."

"Why not?"

"No disrespect, but I thought that was you bruh."

"There ain't nothing wrong with sharing, right?" he asked, and then he paused to wait for me to answer, but I stayed silent because I didn't know where he was going with the question. The look in his eyes was different. He was different, and I felt it.

He said, "I came to talk to you about something." He walked into my office and sat down.

"What's up Clarence?" I asked. His energy was making me feel uncomfortable.

"I don't know brotha. I'm stressing."

"About what?"

"I think my wife is cheating on me." he said. He gave me direct eye contact. His energy was saying a lot, but I kept my composure.

"Wow that's crazy. Why do you think that?"

"I don't know. She is different, and I don't know what to do. I was hoping that you had some suggestions."

"Um, I don't know. Have you tried talking to her?"

"She won't talk to me, and it's killing me. I love her so much and we've been together for almost eleven years. I don't know what I am going to do if she is." he said.

This is the same guy that is messing with women at work and women at the strip club. The same guy who told me what his wife didn't know won't hurt her. I thought.

In my mind, he didn't deserve Angel. The fake, emotional, plea he was giving me was bull. Especially when he knew that he was about to go to his office and let Margo do to him what she was trying to do to me. I knew there was something else going on, but I played along his game.

"What would you do if your wife was cheating on you?" he asked.

"I don't know man. I've never been married." I said.

He shook his head and said, "This is messed up. I never thought she would do me like this. Just the thought of some other man being up in my wife makes me feel crazy."

"That's messed up." I said.

"Anyway, I got to get to my office. Margo is waiting. I can send her back over here when we're done, if you like." he said, and then he smiled.

"Nah I'm good. She said that she was looking for you anyway." I said.

He said, "Yea. Well, don't forget that we got that meeting later."

"Aight."

He stopped at the door and said, "Oh. I forgot to tell you. I will be taking a business trip this weekend, so I will be leaving a little early on Friday. You may be running the staff meeting by yourself."

"That's cool I got it." I said.

"Cool thanks brotha." he said, and then he turned and walked out.

Something about the small talk didn't sit right with me. Clarence had changed. He didn't have the same cheerful attitude that he usually had at work. I turned back to my computer to get back to doing what I was doing before Margo interrupted, and then I thought about how the interaction with her was weird too. I thought about reporting her to human resources for harassment, but part of me felt like Clarence had something to do with it. Margo had flirted with me in the past, but she had never been so forward, and then, for him to show up during her trying to have sex with me, and act so nonchalant about the whole thing. It was almost like he was trying to catch me doing something with her. The entire situation made me feel uncomfortable, and I knew that I needed to get another job as soon as possible. Before Margo walked into my office, I was updating my resume and searching for jobs online. I wasn't happy about giving up my promotion, but I knew that it is for the better. I was not going to continue to work for my future wife's, ex-husband. It was a conflict of interest.

Chapter 23

Royce

There was no breeze, no mosquitos, and no noise. It was a peaceful, warm night in my backyard by the pool with my soon to be wife and mother of my child. The moon was bright and high in the sky, and Angel and I were sitting in my patio chairs talking about our plans. She had on a pair of shorts and a bikini top. I was wearing a pair of swimming trunks without a shirt on. We'd just finished swimming in my pool, and we were drying out. I was drinking a beer and she was sipping on a bottle of water.

She asked, "Do you care if I decorate our new home?"

"I don't care as long as I have my man cave. I am good."

"You already know that you got that."

"You can handle everything else."

"Ok. So, I was thinking about moving here this weekend. Is that too soon?"

"Never too soon. I want you here now."

"Lucky is leaving town for a business trip this weekend, so I planned to leave while he was gone. I think that it would be the perfect time."

"Alright. Do you need my help?"

"No, I got it I'm not taking much. I'm just going to pack and take what is important. Everything else can be replaced. I've already started removing things slowly and putting them in storage. "

"Ok. Cool. Just let me know."

"I will."

"I have a question."

"What?"

"Do you think your husband knows about us?"

"No why?"

"Because we had this weird conversation in my office today."

"Really?

"Yes. He was telling me that you could possibly be cheating on him, and he didn't know what to do. "

"Hmm." she hummed.

"Yea, and what was crazy was he has never talked to me about you, so I just thought that it was strange that he was looking for support from me." I said.

"Maybe he was just trying to confide in you as friend. He has never been the type to tell anyone his business. I mean, he has really got his nerve to be talking about me with all the women he runs around with."

"Yea, and right before he showed up in my office, one of the girls that works there tried to come on to me. I wouldn't be surprised if he sent her in there."

"Are you serious?"

"Yea."

"That is crazy. Are you going to report her?"

"I thought about it, but I'm just going to do everything I can to get out of there quickly. You just worry about moving here this weekend. I'm ready to get him out of both of our lives."

"Well, after he sees that I am gone, he will know that we are over and there is no turning back."

I reached over and touched her small baby bump. It wasn't big enough for a person to detect a pregnancy when she had clothes on, but when she was undressed it was noticeable. I wasn't sure how she had been hiding it from her husband. I did notice that she was wearing loose fitted clothing more often. I could only imagine that she did the same when she was at home. By that time, I was ready to have my future wife at home with me, so I could wake up to her every day, and watch my baby grow inside of her. I was ready for Clarence to be out of the picture, so I could have Angel all to myself.

I said, "I can't wait for you to be all mine."

"I'm finally going to be all yours."

I stood up grabbed her hand and helped her stand up, and then she followed me back inside of my house.

Chapter 24

Angel

Angel walked into her house after work thinking that it was the last day that she would have to share a home with her husband Lucky. Angel took off her shoes and walked barefoot to the guest bedroom. She put her shoes on the floor by the dresser in the bedroom, and then she walked towards the den. She could hear Lucky walking down the stairs, but she didn't speak. Angel just kept walking.

"How was work today?" Lucky asked as he followed Angel into their den. Angel silently wished that she would've just left her alone and let her go to bed without them speaking a word to each other.

"It was fine." she said coldly.

"You don't have to talk to me like that." he said.

"Talk to you like what?" she asked.

"Emotionless like you can't stand me."

She turned to face him. "What do you want?"

"I want my wife to talk to me like she used to, touch me like she used to, and love me like she used to."

"That ship has sailed." she said.

"Who is he?" Lucky asked.

"Who is what?"

"The mutha fucka that got you acting like that."

"I don't know what you're talking about."

"Angel don't lie to me." Clarence said angrily. He moved closer to her.

"Lucky, move. What is your problem?"

"Don't tell me to move. I want to hear the truth from your mouth!"

"Why are you yelling? There is nothing to tell."

"*Oh, there is a lot* to tell Angel." he said sarcastically.

"I'm not in the mood for this Lucky."

"We can start by talking about the fact that I have followed you for the last five days."

Angel made a screwed face. She was stunned. Angel's first thought was that Lucky couldn't be serious. She had never been followed in her life.

"You followed me?" she asked.

"Yea."

"What the hell were you doing following me Lucky?"

"Because I needed to see for myself."

"See what?" Angel stepped away from him.

"I needed to see who the hell was pulling you away from me."

"You should not have been following me." Angel said angrily.

"Why? Because you didn't want me to know about Royce right!" he yelled and stepped closer to her.

Angel side stepped him. "I don't have time for this, so I'm going to leave." she said, and then she started walking through the hallway. Lucky followed her still yelling.

"You want to leave before you tell me why you're cheating on me with my coworker!" Lucky yelled.

"Leave me alone Lucky."

"I watched you go into his house every day and come out with a smile on your face! Do you know how that made me feel!? Royce! Royce of all people!? How long have you been doing this behind my back!? Since the Super Bowl party!?"

"No." she said. She slid her shoes back on, and then she made her way to the door.

"Angel, you're not going anywhere! We are going to talk about this!" Lucky said as he stepped in front of the door.

"Lucky you need to let me leave."

"No, you're not leaving. We need to talk about this. I want to know why!?"

"I don't owe you an explanation! I told you that I was done with this marriage! There is nothing else to say!"

"It's been ten years, and this is what it has come to!? You messing around with someone I know!? Basically, my friend!"

"You have been cheating on me for years!"

"So, that gives you the right to mess around with someone else!"

"I just want to go Lucky."

"So, you can go back over there with him? Hell no! As a matter, of fact. Come here. I'm gonna make love to my wife." Lucky grabbed her arm and pulled her to him. Angel started struggling with him.

"No, you're not!"

"Yes, I am." Lucky said as Angel continued to struggle to get out of his grip. He got frustrated and started pulling her down the hallway towards the guest bedroom.

"Lucky stop!" Angel yelled as he was pulling her down the hallway.

"No! You stop!" Lucky yelled.

Angel continued to struggle with him. She swung and hit him in the face. Lucky let go of her and grabbed his face, and then he swung and punched Angel so hard that she fell to the floor. She yelped and grabbed her face, and then he punched her again before kicking her in the stomach.

"Lucky no!" she cried out as she curled up to protect her pregnant belly.

"Now look what you made me do Angel! Fuck!" he yelled.

He put his hands on his head as he paced the floor a couple of times. He stopped pacing and scooped her up off the floor. Angel started yelling and fighting to get away again. She landed a punch to his head. Lucky fought with her a little, and then he slammed her up against the wall. He hit her in the face again, and then she screamed, but she wasn't giving up the fight.

"Stop Angel!" he yelled.

She kept swinging, so he tussled with her until she kicked him in his manhood and took off running. He grabbed himself, and then he chased her through the house.

When he caught up to her, he was furious. He grabbed the back of her shirt and snatched her back to him. She lost her balance and fell to the floor. Lucky began dragging her back through the hallway by her shirt. She screamed and continued to struggle the entire way back through the hallway towards the bedroom. He let her go, stepped over her, hit her again, and then she stopped moving. Lucky noticed that she had stopped moving, so he called her name.

"Angel." he said as he shook her.

Angel didn't respond. She was lying still with her eyes closed. He shook her again, but she didn't move. Lucky repeated her name, when she didn't move, he calmly picked her up and put her over his shoulder. He walked into the bedroom, laid her on the guest bed, pushed her dress up, and pulled her panties to the side. Angel regained consciousness, realized what Lucky was doing, and began to yell.

"Stop Lucky!"

She started squirming and kicking to try to stop him from entering her, but he pinned her hands to the bed, dodged the kicks, and spread her legs open.

"Quit fighting me Angel. I love you. This been mine for eleven years." he said.

He leaned down to kiss her, but she turned her head to the side. The kiss landed on her cheek. She continued to cry, but she had no control and she couldn't stop him. Lucky pushed his manhood inside of her and told her that he loved her.

"I love you baby." he whispered.

Angel said, "I don't want to do this."

"You have no choice." Lucky said.

"Lucky please stop." she cried.

Lucky became angry again and asked, "Why? Because of Royce?

"Please Lucky." Angel pleaded.

She didn't want to have sex with Lucky. She was pregnant with another man's baby. The man that she loved. Having sex with Lucky was the last thing she wanted to do. She fought hard to stop him because she didn't want to feel him inside of her. She had given her heart and her body to Royce. Lucky was no longer welcome.

Lucky grabbed her neck and said, "You got one fucked up, if you think I'm gonna let you walk out of my life and into the arms of another man!"

Lucky continued squeezing her neck, and he was squeezing so tight Angel couldn't breathe. Tears were running down her face and her lips were moving but no words were coming out. She was trying to tell him that she couldn't breathe, but he wasn't letting go. He continued to squeeze her neck and make love to her. Eventually, Angel's lips stopped moving and her body went limp, but Lucky didn't stop until he got his. After Lucky busted, he realized that she wasn't moving at all. Lucky let go of her and called her name again. She didn't say anything, so he pulled out of her and stepped back. He repeated her name, but she didn't move, so he scooped her up into his arms.

"I love you Angel." he whispered, and then he carried her out of the room.

Chapter 25

Royce

I text messaged Angel to see if she was sure that she didn't need my help moving some of her stuff to my house. She didn't respond right away, but it was normal for her to wait until she got to her office. Both of us were usually up before the crack of dawn to go to work, so she would send me a text message once she was settled in at her office. The only thing that was abnormal to me was that she didn't send me her usual goodnight text, but I brushed that off. I knew that after the work day was done, she was going to be all mine forever.

I stood in my full-length mirror buttoning up my white shirt. I put on a silk tie that had hues of red, black, and, grey on it. I used my lint brush on my charcoal grey pants, sprayed on a little cologne, and put my silver watch on. I put my wallet in my back pocket and picked up my keys from my dresser. I walked down the stairs to my front door, and then I remembered that I wanted to wear my new shades, so I walked back through my house to the kitchen table to get them. I walked back to the door, opened it, and walked out into the morning sun.

As soon as I walked out, I got hit in the face. I grabbed my face and looked back to see who it was. I saw a two, big, husky, masked men, dressed in all-black sweat suits. I started swinging punches. They were trying to grab me as I fought back, but I was putting up a fight. I hit one in the face a couple of times, and the other in the stomach.

They stopped trying to grab me and started swinging. I was dodging punches left and right and swinging back. I don't think they anticipated being up against a trained fighter. I'd been training at a gym for years, and I was fighting for my life in a GQ magazine outfit. They hit me a couple of times, but I kept swinging. I was connecting punches like I was Mayweather. I guess one of the men got tired of fighting me, and the next thing I heard was what sounded like a firecracker.

Pow!

I grabbed my stomach and went down. I heard one of them say, "Let's go!"

They took off running and jumped into a vehicle. I heard the tires screech against the pavement as they pulled off. I looked down and saw my blood soaking my shirt. I started trying to get back to my door to go into my house, but I couldn't seem to get there. I dropped to my knees still holding my wound, and then I laid down and rolled onto my back. A few of my neighbors ran out of their houses towards me.

"Oh, my God. Sir are you ok?" I heard one of the ladies say.

"Honey, call 911!" I heard another lady tell her husband.

"Stay with us sir." The guy with the phone said.

"Can you tell me your name?" The guy asked.

"Royce."

"Ok. Yes. He is my neighbor. I think that he has been shot. There is a lot of blood. He is still alive and breathing. He said his name is Royce. Please hurry." the guy said into his cell phone.

I still had my hand on my wound, but I was fading. Everything was starting to get dark. The concerned look in my neighbor's eyes was vanishing slowly as I tried to cling to life.

"Royce help is on the way. Stay with us." the man said.

"Do you know who did this to you?" One of the ladies asked.

I shook my head no. I heard sirens in the distance. I looked up at the palm tree above me and the blue skies. I prayed to God that I would live, and then I blacked out.

To be continued……

Contact

Email: niarichbooks@gmail.com

Available Now

Available Now

Nia Rich

Lovers Remorse